THE TWILIGHTERS
ROAD TRIP

Thor Wesenlund

Bayview Publishing Qld

Book Cover by Bayview Publishing Australia

Illustrations by Sandy Freeleagus

Edition One 2025

Contents

Prologue

The Twilighters Road Trip

Book one in the series

These two guys and their friends are true characters of a bygone era in Australia. They come from a special breed of veterans as submariners. Their lives had posed a series of experiences that helped shape their outlook life. Lofty and Tezza are no longer young men but they are still capable of mischief and rebellion against authority. They have worked hard and achieved a good life for themselves and their families and have nothing to apologise for. These guys are rascals like many submariners of their era, but they are not ready to slow down or follow the normal retirement path.

There is also a happy side to their lives, which comes from growing up in the carefree, uncomplicated and happy society that they knew in the 1950's and 60's. Have they been able to endure changes in society knowing that the less demanding character hidden inside each of them is only expressed when they are with their close friends of the same ilk. Maybe but they see themselves fortunate to be able to share their expeiences and many adventures with others.

Some of their attitudes and ramblings may shock readers but they are the honest exchanges that a lot of older men and vets express to each other. They are definitely not WOKE so be warned if you are easily offended. Ask any veteran, especially ex submariners, about some of the tales in this book and they will tell you in matter-of-fact terms.

"Been there, done that"

This particular book is based on a memorable road trip I took with my lifelong friend and fellow conspiritor Terry Rowell who subsequently inspired me to write this book. Also thanks to my good friend and wonderful Artist Sandy Freeleagus whoes drawings are throughout this book and the others in the series. To all those mates that added colur and flavour to my life, thankyou for your support and encouragemnt throughout the years.

To all those still enjoying their later years and as they approach the end of lifes conveyor can you say you had a good life and grew old disgracefully and with honour. Perhaps the young ones that follow us will understand our logic and the spirit that made our lives so full and enjoyable despite the hardships many of us faced and the sacrifices made by many in the past. I hope this book brings back some memories and misadventures and at least puts a smile on your face occassionally.

THE TWILIGHT RETIREMENT RESORT

The Sunnyvale Twilight retirement resort is an up-market retirement village with neat rows of manufactured bungalows and well-kept gardens on the outskirts of the city. There are plenty of things to do if you like bowls, bingo and card games. Sunyvale had the usual facilities like a swimming pool and community hall, a small cafe and dining area as well as an attached aged care facility where you were supposed to go when you could no longer look after yourself.

John Tezzman known to most as Tezza and Brad Loftgren known as Lofty (the lads) had called Sunnyvale their home for the past couple of years. The two lifelong friends from their days as submariners had been relocated from their homes to Sunnyvales Twilight Retirement Village at their wives insistence. Neither were happy about the idea and rebelled against the authoritarian management at Sunnyvale on a regular basis

THE CEREMONY

Today was a special occasion at The Twilight village. It was the dedication ceremony for a new gym extension and as usual the local politicians and hangers on wanted to get their smell on it despite not having contributed a cent to the thing. The lads had been under strict orders to behave and close observation to ensure none of their regular mischief could take place.

At 11am the residents gathered in the community hall to listen to speeches and dutifully clap. The lads were made to sit at the back of the hall under the watchful eye of one of the managers goons.

Sandy had called in sick whilst his wife was away visiting friends interstate. The scene was set with pictures of the work progressing on a big screen behind a lectern and an electronic screen on the front of it. The idiot manager had done his usual patronizing welcome to residents finishing with the customary finger thing that all were supposed to do when he announced.

'How do Twilighters say hello'

Lofty and Tezza gave him the bird with Tezza whispering to Lofty, "why do they put up with that fucking idiot"

Lofty nods and says, "he used to run a youth detention Centre I think"

They both giggled quietly as the managers lackey behind them says

"shush, show some respect for the colonel"

It was true the Twilight manager was a retired Army Colonel from the catering branch and he hated Navy types which put the lads in his sights for anything and everything he could throw at them.

Let the pranking begin

It was customary to play a triumphal march as the dignitaries and officials entered from the back and walked in regal procession to take their places on the stage. However, something went wrong and a rude version of send in the clowns blared out with much laughter and giggling whilst the Sunnyvale lackey behind the two lads frisked them only to find nothing.

The Twilight Village general manager stood up to the lectern and made his opening remarks. The screen on the front of the lectern lit up with his name and title then went blank and the word WANKA came on.

He could not see the screen below and in front of the lectern as he continued in earnest as the residents giggled and his lackey behind the two lads waved vigorously to the Colonel who avoided the gesturing and continued thinking his usual bad jokes were goind down well with the residents and guests.

The big screen behind him then changed to show him in a naked embrace with his secretary and some desk top love making. The residents began to laugh aloud but the screen went dead before he could turn around and see what was on it.

Each speech was treated with the same irreverence and many of the residents later said it was the most entertainment they had ever had. Especially the snapshots of the local politician doing his thing in the park toilets and the nursing home matron on her knees in front of a grateful doctor.

After the ceremony and many apologies, the lads were asked to come to the main office and were questioned whilst their homes were searched. The Manager of Twilight Vilage went so far as to get the local police involved but nothing was found that could be connected to the lads and the actual video was also missing.

Tezza and Lofty had sat listening to the tirade of abuse and language coming from the assembled dignitaries as questions were fired at the lads, but nothing could be found that caused the problems. This was not enough to appease the Manager.

"I know this is your doing and when I find out how you did it I will kick you both out of here and make sure your charged with something" says the Manager glaring at the two lads as Tezza blows him a kiss.

"Public airing would suit us chief truth can be a bit damaging to reputations, I guess. I wonder what the owners of this place would say. Maybe they should get to see the performance" says Tezza,

Glowing with anger the manager tells the lads to get out.

Wheeling down the road in their golf cart Tezza turns to Lofty smiling.

"That went well mate. Shame we couldn't stick around to see how the dignitaries special laxative coffee went down Anyway; we had better catch up with Sandy and disarm all that stuff before they search his place. Bloody brilliant though wasn't it" says Tezza.

"Yep, up there with one of our better pranks and Im sure it will have lasting effects judging by the dignitaries clutching their stomachs as we left." says Lofty

Tezza was deep in thought as they arrived at Sandys place to find him heading out in his car.

"Sorry guys, got to go and get this satellite stuff back to my mate. The tapes are in the garden safe which I will move later."

There wasn't much to say as Sandy sped off down the road. They had done this before and getting rid of the evidence was all part of the plan.

Back at Tezza's place the pair sat on the back deck and reminisced about the past. Tezza had a thought.

"Mate I was thinking of the adventures we've had and the mayhem its caused. Maybe it's time we got out of here till things calm down. What about we do a road trip to one of the navy reunions we never seem to get to. Theres, one coming up soon. The ladies always used enjoyed them and it would make for some fun along the way." Says Tezza

"Great idea, it will be good to be on the road again. let's see if Sandy wants in and then we can sort out the details" says Lofty

MISCHIEF

Lofty and Tezza had agreed to move to The Twilight Village on the condition that they could be somewhere near each other. Now living next door to each other and with another old rascal either side the pair often pranked the management and others Their wives were aware of mischiefs, but they had plenty of bingo, yoga, cards and other stuff to keep them busy and entertained so they just ignored the issue.

In fact, they had decided if worse came to worse and the men were asked to leave, they would try and stay in one of the two houses. Tezza and Lofty were never happy at Twilights but despite being aware of the strict controls imposed they managed to create mischief and disrupt events with hilarious outcomes. They had become legends amongst many of the residents, who enjoyed their frequent additions to signs at the front gates. The management were not as impressed and had sought to have them evicted but they could never actually pin any incident or mishap on them.

SANDY

A friend from their Submaring days, Lee Freeman, lived on the other side of Lofty and was a frequent co-conspirator in their mischief. known as Sandy due to the desert he created as a front garden which annoyed the management who regularly drove past in their golf carts to tut, tut and point. Sandy was an electronics guru and had installed a talking and singing rocks that were carefully disguised and would tell those who came too close to fuck off.

They were difficult to spot and the sensors were well hidden and the sound came from a distant rock speaker that was automatically changed. This made finding the origin and outputs vey diffucult. Occasionally, late at night the rock would burst into song and sing a horse with no name song. Sandy reckoned this matched his garden, which resembled a desert scene with cactus and rocks and sand as opposed to the neat roses and flower beds of his neighbors.

It greatly annoyed management, but it was clear in the body Corporate rules that he cold do it. The rules said that you could have whatever you wanted in your garden. That hadn't stopped them trying to get it changed but with little or no success. The talking and singing rock were frequently moved so efforts to find it proved fruitless and frustrating for the gardeners sent to pull it out of Sandys Garden who would turn on the sprinklers remotely whenever they tried

The three men had developed outside interests as well as harassing the patronising management that spoke to the residents like 5-year-olds.

Tezza had interests in greyhounds at a local breeding and racing farm and Lofty had moved his extensive workshop to a nearby factory unit where he and Sandy would escape to play with vehicles and carry out experiments.

Sandy was also a very good cartoonist and would lampoon the management and some of the residents by secretly placing a cartoon alongside some the management edicts on the noticeboard or with Lofties help inserting it into the Sunnyvale website unseen.

It had become a favourite for most residents to see what the phantom cartoonist had to say each week. Even though the management of Twilight villagee had their suspicions about who was doing it they never managed to pin the blame on Sandy, who they just saw as an eccentric old fool.

Lofty and Tezza often got away with things by using a walking frame in Tezza's case and walking stick in Lofty's case, even though neither needed them. The apparatus had become a means of transporting mischief like Sandys cartoons and hiding nips of rum and other bits of mischief.

They were often the first to be questioned by management after something went wrong but always had an alibi using their mobility issues to explain that it couldn't have been them. In fact, there was nothing wrong with their fitness for their age and away from the glare of the Sunnyvale management they we all three very active.

Their wives of course knew of their extra curricula activities but turned a blind eye so long as they were not blamed for the misadventures. In part the management and others sympathized with the women for having to put up with the three lunatics.

MISBEHAVING

Past mischiefs included spiking the Christmas punch bowl which led to naked dancing and rude singing. The annual fireworks display that somehow wound up with military grade rockets and flares decimating the duck pond. Then there was the annual golf cart parade that somehow saw the towed floats distributing bad smells as they went along.

Of course, the more subtle things like changing the welcome to Twilight Resort electronic sign at the entrance to read 'Piss off while you can' and 'Pensioner Detention Centre'. The spiking of the coffee shop tea and coffee grounds with marijuana was perhaps the last event that saw very unusual behavior by the regulars.

So, whilst nothing could be proved it was always clear to the management and many of the residents who was responsible.

The three old rascals really didn't want to be there, but their wives insistence mandated their stay and to some extent their health and fitness meant they seemed to rely on others for major tasks and chores. Some thought the three old rascals were fooling and were in fact much more able than they made out. The truth is both their health and mental capacities were fine, but they liked to give the impression that it wouldn't be long before they were both nursing home residents and occupiers of woolly armchairs.

Lofty and Sandy had set up elaborate secret panels in their back fences which allowed them to slip unseen into the wooded area behind the resort. Sandys love of gadgets had also provided remotely operated tapes that played when the lads were out on one of their forays and gave the impression of someone being home.

Much of their electronic and other mischief making gear was hidden in panels behind the broom cupboards so the wives never knew they existed. All this technology allowed the 3 amigos to come and go unseen except for Tezza's 82 year old neighbor, who was regularly bribed with pastries and bourbon to buy his silence. This neighbor often supported the lads pranks as he was not a fan of the Colonel, as the Manager of the resort preferred to be called, who ran the place like a military prison camp.

ROAD TRIP CONSPIRACY

The idea of the road trip had gelled in Tezzas mind some time ago. Now it seemed like a good time to get out of the place and let the heat die down. It was also a way to get out of the Twilight zone as Lofty called the place. It was also time for them to have some fun whilst making the women folk happy at the same time. The reunion function next month seemed like a good excuse and so the thought progressed.

Discussions with Sandy revealed he was going to visit one of his sons and then fly to the reunion so unfortunately, he could not join them for the road trip but he promised to get back to them on the idea.

Discussions with the wives revealed a hint of suspicion regarding the separate travel arrangements to the reunion but general accord with the idea. In a pleading voice the two men explained the long history they had together and played up their health issues with hang dog expressions.

"You know Tezza and I go back a long way, and I don't need to tell you our health is on the decline", says Lofty in a convincing voice with theatrical pauses that fooled neither women.

"We would like to spend a few days of quality time together before, well you know". continues Tezza,

"I know I promised you a trip away together, but Tezza and I were talking and unbelievably we both got very teary and something inside both of us said that we should not miss this opportunity, what do you think. Besides we can have a good time at the reunion."

It appeared a chord was struck and the plan was hatched with unanimous agreement and the 4 were set for the road trip. The plan was based on a bonding trip for Lofty and Tezza whilst the ladies could enjoy some girl time to themselves in a posh hotel. The ladies would fly to the reunion whilst Tezza and Lofty would drive north supposedly in Loftys small SUV. The ladies agreed it was the way to go and the men earned some bonus bedroom points to be redeemed later. Claps and laughter from the two women said it all with the two women scurrying away to plan their wardrobe and accommodation.

"This is going to cost us you know Tezza," says Lofty

"I guess so but look on it as an investment," replied Tezza

"How so" says Lofty looking puzzled

"Well, for a start we can have some fun on the road without the female handbrakes and speed regulators. We also get away from here before it gets too hot after the recent prank which they're certain to try and pin on us. Then of course theirs the bonus bedroom points."

"I guess everything has a cost" says Lofty smiling at the thought of freedom.

The pair of old larrikins looked over maps and brochures and planned their trip with great enthusiasm and joy.

Lofty and Tezza had shared some very good times together, albeit many years ago before they both married, with the last few years having been spent in the Twilight Retirement Resort which had brought little joy to them. However, the ladies were both content and turned a blind eye to their men's external activities but were not too happy with the sympathetic reception they always got with reference to their larrikin husbands. They explained it away as a hangover from their service experiences and PTSD which seemed to satisfy some whilst others commented they should be put away.

Both men agreed it would be fun to stroll down memory lane as they went down the road together. So, the die was cast and another adventure for the two old friends was about to begin. Tezza, in his usual organised way, took charge of most of the arrangements as was his experience as a Coxswain in the Navy. Lofty was just happy to be going and took it all in his stride.

CHARIOT OF FIRE

It was very early in the day and the ladies had barely left for the airport when Lofty ushered Tezza out to the back fence and through the secret flip panel. Their usual escape to the workshop was via a shallow drainage ditch at the edge of the forest that shielded the retirement village from a main road.

The shallow culvert emerged at the end of the industrial park which meant they would come and go unseen. Today was no different as they opened the roller door and went into Lofty and Sandys man cave at the factory unit. With a flourishing stroke of his hand, Lofty pulls old bed sheets off his and Sandys latest creation.

"What the ."... Says Tezza

"This is our ride for the road trip, isn't she a beaut." says Lofty.

"Lofty, Lofty, Lofty, it's a marvelous creation, whatever it is, but I thought we agreed we were taking your Prius."

Smiling broadly Lofty winks,

"No that's just a story for her benefit. This little beauty needs its legs stretched and is way more capable than that little rice burner. Besides Sandy is looking after the Prius whilst his car is getting sorted." says Lofty

"OK, I'll bite, where do you wind it up and how often." says Tezza

"You've lost your sense of adventure Tezza. Just wait till you see the features of this fine automobile" says Lofty with another flourish that would have made a game show host proud as he walked Tezza around the beast.

Tezza took it all in, thinking Lofty has come up with some great follies in the past but he does have an engineering brain so Ill amuse him before I hire us a car or we get arrested for disturbing the peace with this monster.

The thing was enormous and Tezza was impressed but a bit worried that Lofty had intentions of running the monster on the road trip to the reunion. The bonnet must have been 10ft long and the rear wagon section was very ornate but didn't look like it belonged to the vehicle. The wheels were also kind of weird and the back doors didn't have any handles. Tezza also noticed it was registered in another state. He was beginning to get a bad feeling about this.

Lofty kicked a milk crate over to the passenger door and wrenched it open for Tezza to climb in.

"Well, what you think," says Lofty.

"It's very different "says Tezza with a frown on his face.

"Let me run you through some of the controls we've fitted" says Lofty as he explains the controls and functions.

"I built this little beauty from the bones of a Romanian car, the Goolag Mk4. Very famous Lithuanian designer put these together for the Russian army as troop carriers but it failed to meet their requirements. Seems like it was a bit noisy and harsh riding to the point that on trials some of the troops were injured bouncing around in the back. Anyway, I found it near a swamp being used to hunt crocs and shipped it here."

"Hold on, so you're asking me to go north in some failed Russian experiment that injured people and was so noisy the enemy could hear it from miles away. Are you mad, no wait we know you're mad, am I mad then?" says Tezza looking in the enormous rear view mirror,

Not to be put off Lofty enthusiastically continues.

"Right, so here you have the control yoke which I got from my mate at aviation spares. Couldn't find a steering wheel to fit but this works fine. You'll get used to the gauges. The altimeter is a revs gauge and angle and bank is the fuel gauge" and so Lofty went on with his explanations until Tezza holds up his hands.

"Wait a minute. So all the instruments are converted aircraft spares right? Then what's that bloody big brass steam gauge there in the middle of the dash?" says Tezza.

"Temperature of course what else?" says Lofty looking incredulously at Tezza moving on to explain the engine is a 6 litre diesel with......until Tezza stops him again

"STOP right there. 6 litre diesel!! Have you bought shares in a fuel company or something. It's going to cost a bloody fortune to run this tank up to where we are going." says Tezza

"No No No! This beasty runs on anything oily. Now I'm using cooking oil from the local chippy mixed with some diesel and just a touch of waste lube oil from the local garage. It's got a 190 litre tank and I've added a 50 litre auxiliary". Says Lofty with a wave of his hand and proud smile on his face.

"Great, so all we need to do when we stop for lunch is to ask the cafe guy for the left-over oil from his deep fat fryer." says Tezza

"Got it in one ole son, I've even rigged up a transfer pump in the back there" says Lofty pointing to a lump of war surplus machinery.

"While we are at it, the back of this thing looks very ornate but why don't the back doors open?" says Tezza

"Ah!, you've spotted the small design error. It appears that because the vehicle is so long it flexes a bit and the back doors kept flying open when I went around corners. Gave a few pedestrians a bit of fright and I nearly lost the mother-in-law out the back door once. So now I've tied them up so they can't open." Says Lofty

"OK sounds like one of your creations, but what about the ornate rear end. ´ says Tezza

"Now that's an interesting story. I picked it up from a wrecker who was into old army stuff and swapped me the back of a hearse for the troop carrier bit. Looks pretty good eh!" Says Lofty with a proud grin on his face.

So, let me get this straight , I'm going north in a 6 litre waste oil burning hearse that you've built...Not fucking likely Lofty, I'm calling the hire car company says Tezza struggling with the door.

"Wait before you do that, let me take you for a run and if you're still hesitant I will get the hire car OK," says Lofty.

Tezza thought for a moment.

"OK I grant you the thing is quite comfortable once you get in and there is plenty of room for our stuff but I'm not sleeping back there in case you have that idea," says Tezza with stern look on his face

With the workshop door open Lofty hits the ignition. There's an loud whining sound coming from the engine as Lofty pumps the pedals and pulls switches. Takes a while to kick over when she's cold, it's the air start you can hear yells Lofty over the din.

There's a huge rumble as the thing shudders into life and clouds of smoke billow out into the industrial estate. A crunch of gears and the behemoth lumbers out of the garage and onto the quiet streets. Tezza hangs on for grim death as they hurtle down the laneway and onto the main road.

As they come to the first corner. They launch into a sharp right hand corner with clouds of smoke billowing behind them and the distinct smell of fish and chips pervading everything. The car seems to float around the corner despite leaning over at a sickening angle. Lofty is smiling his head off and looks across at Tezza for recognition of his mastery of the behemoth

"It's the aircraft tyres on the back that make it float," yells Lofty over the dim having seen the look of terror on Tezza's face. As he shuffles a gear or 2 and the big engine accelerates the thing onto a highway.

"I'll show you how she goes on the highway" yells Lofty over the din as the monster roars down the road past startled motorists and a bus stop filled with people who will smell like a fish and chip shop for the rest of the day.

"OK, OK, you've proved you point let's just put the bloody thing away Ill change my undies and get a hire car." says Tezza urgently

"Ok but first we need to do a lap around Twilight resort and show Sandy as well as wake up the Twilighters," say Lofty

"No mate you can't do that," says Tezza but it was too late as they careered through the main gate with Lofty pushing a big gate opening button and flicking the switch for the aircraft landing lights that were strong enough to melt the tarmac and set fire to bushes.

Down the main street of the resort, they roared with clouds of acrid smoke blanketing the whole area. Sandy was out the front and waved and cheered as they passed leaving him in a cloud of smoke laughing and coughing at the same time whilst his wife dragged him inside.

Accelerating down the exit road past the administration building Lofty sets the fuel mixture to rich and thick clouds of smoke mask their exit and settle over the main buildings as they hurtle out the main gate and onto the road again.

"Okay you've had your fun now before we get arrested let's put this thing away and pretend like it wasn't us." says Tezza,

"Too late" says Lofty as a Blue and Red flashing light reflects in the rear vision mirror.

"Shit, its Polly" says Lofty,

"Who the fuck is Polly"? Says Tezza

"He's a highway patrol mate of mine, ex-Navy, who rode bikes with me and a bunch of other idiots. He's a family friend and he told me not to get this thing out again until it passes a road worthy. Says Lofty opening his window as Polly approaches

"Lofty, your missus warned me that you might get this thing out whilst she was away, and you know my thoughts on this monstrosity. Now, this is the final warning, take the bastard thing back to the garage and lock it up. I'm going to follow you so don't try sneaking off with some lame excuse like last time.

Lofty snaps off a salute and half closes the window muttering to himself about justice and no sense of adventure.

Feeling suitably admonished but spiteful, Lofty puts the monster into gear and with the mixture still rich and the clutch in, Lofty revs the engine filling the air with clouds of putrid smoke which also fills Polly's patrol car parked behind.

"Sorry," says Lofty with his head out the window smiling as he did so.

"You really like to push the envelope, don't you Lofty" says Tezza as they trundle back into the workshop with a police escort.

Getting out of the beast they notice that the acrid smoke was still hanging around and multiple car alarms where wailing in chorus through the normally quite suburb. Seeing Tezza's concern Lofty answers the unspoken question.

"It's the vibrations from the engine; it always sets off the car alarms and some dogs as well. said Lofty

"The neighbors must really love you Lofty" says Tezza.

"Yep, I've had the odd run in with the wowsers who accuse me of turning the resort into an industrial estate, but it's the firemen that get upset the most when they keep getting called out to an industrial fire only to find I'm just tuning up the engine or trying a new fuel." said Lofty

Climbing down, Lofty apologises to Polly and makes sure he doesn't let the Twilight gestapo know about their little run. Meantime Tezza's has phoned a hire car company. Muttering to himself, mad old bastard he should have been a bloody stoker, referring to his love of machinery which was the opposite of his job in the Navy.

(footnote- Stoker is a sailor's term for engine room folk)

Sneaking back into Lofty's house through the back fences secret gate, they quickly don their usual tracksuit and get their walking stick and frame props and head out to the front of the house. A stinking haze still hung over the street as the residents gathered and muttered about the smell.

Through the gloom the lads saw the headlights and flashing lights of the Colonels golf cart approaching. Pulling up in front of the lads the overweight colonel and his minion dismount and confront them pointing to the haze.

"I just know you two had something to do with this and when I find out you're both out of here." Says the Colonal

"Fair go Colonel Blimp, we've been here packing for our trip, right Tezza." says Lofty, with Tezza nodding and smiling agreement whilst their friendly neighbour speaks up:

"They have been in all morning and it was probably a dodgy garbage truck or something" he says

Still not convinced the Colonel stomps off with a parting comment that he will be back and his name is Blum not blimp.

Back inside the lads and the neighbour celebrate with a high five and glass of scotch to mark the occasion of another sortie successfully carried out.

Later when the ladies get home the lads are fast asleep on the lounge having cleaned up half a bottle of scotch with the neighbour who was also flaking out in a chair.

Suspecting the smell and the haze has something to do with these two old fools, the ladies decide to leave sleeping dogs lay and headed off to Tezza's house to discuss the trip. The lads managed to avoid the colonel and his minions for the rest of the time before departing and made sure their departure was very early and with minimum noise or fuss.

HEADING NORTH

The sun was barely up in the sky as the hire car with its 2 aged occupants slipped its suburban berth and headed north. Two old mates were on a road trip down a path of memories and fun and to visit old friends on their way to the annual submariners convention some 1200kms away in the tropical north.

Not a small journey thought Lofty sitting disgruntled behind the wheel of the hire car having had to leave his marvelous creation in the workshop, but both were pleased that they'd been able to persuade their wives to fly whilst they relived their youthful exploits and caught up with where each of their lives had led them.

What would they find on this journey of discovery and why were they doing it. After all, neither of them was getting any younger and both had conspired to make this journey knowing that it may be their last together. Lofty had a few heart problems and Tezza's health was none to good either. Not to mention that both were retired now and there was pressure from their wives to slow down and stop their adventures.

How had their lives developed over the years, had their individual philosophies on life changed, what of the future and many other questions flashed through each of their minds as they headed north.

This would become a theme for many discussions as the trip progressed with neither really knowing what the outcome would be or what surprises might be revealed. However, both were certain in the knowledge that this trip was going to be a good one. So the adventure began with a common unspoken word with looks and smiles exchanged. They were on their way.

Tezza was thinking of the times they had seen and a few of their more intrepid adventures in worse vehicles than this in their younger days, but it was nice to be comfortably seated in a reasonable car that suited the purpose he thought.

As the car slipped down the entrance to the main freeway north, Tezza's mind was wandering back to the days he Lofty had seen in their youth. The sun shone brightly through the windscreen as the traffic snarls of suburbia faded behind them and the car picked up speed.

The car slid effortlessly past a row of trucks and a couple of caravans as Lofty swung the car back into the left-hand lane to let a fast-approaching sports car past, muttering to himself. "Fucking idiot" still miffed at not being able to take his beast. Tezza thinks he seems to swear a lot more these days realizing that they had hardly spoken since fighting their way out of Sydney except for the usual grumbles about traffic, wives and their favourite football team the west Tigers.

"Well, here we are old friend" says Tezza looking sideways at a smiling Lofty who was thinking to himself this is what we've needed for a long time I reckon. Sliding down the highway at a good clip, the conversation quickly turned to a battered old Holden that Tezza's brother had lent him so they could commute to a distant base they were both posted to. The stories began to flow back and forth, and it was hard for either one to focus on one period.

This was going to be a road trip to remember. A road trip, back to the age of reason, or the lack of it, was the agreed chant for the trip.

LONG MARRIAGE PHILOSOPHY

With the look of wisdom on his face Tezza breaks the silence again.

"Have you ever thought how we have both managed to stay married for so long and is there a magic plan that we should let other husbands know about "

Looking bemused Lofty acknowledge the start of discussions

"I have a feeling you are about to unload one of your philosophical loads of clap trap, but if it helps you to cleanse your soul, go for it". Exclaimed Lofty

Waving Lofty's comments away Tezza continues his thoughts

"Don't be too quick to dismiss my findings on marriage. There is some proof of that sitting in this car. The basic rules are quite straight forward.

To graduate from husband school and be fully qualified according to the book you must have saved yourself up for your wife on their wedding day, must not drink anything stronger than lemonade, must not have a dollar or two hidden in the wallet, and must love kids even though they are not yours."

"Wait up, you're trying to say those are my traits and background" says Lofty looking angry

"If the shoe fits cinders." Says Tezza smiling

"Sorry to burst your bubble chief but I wouldn't qualify for any of those things and you certainly don't" says Lofty

"It's just a checklist so let me finish. The ideal husband must love housework and be home at 6 o'clock every day. Then they must go grocery shopping with the love of their life, dressed to the standard that would be appropriate to go to a wedding, with no thongs, sandals, or comfortable tracksuits.

"Then, to show she is boss, she will purchase at least 6 women's magazines, placed strategically so the whole shopping center can read the headlines and stare at the husband pushing the trolley."

It was clear that Lofty was deep in thought and probably ticking off points in his memory. Tezza knew once Lofty got into this state he had won and it was time to change the subject, knowing that he would likely bring the subject back up later.

"Lofty, I'm sure you're on the same wavelength as me regarding long marriage management, for me it meant not seeing her for long periods. If I were lucky enough to spend between 6 and 9 months a year at sea Id have complete peace. My get away from her meant no arguing, and no visiting her family and so many more things that could be avoided.

"Get away from the rug rats, no travelling more miles than necessary on a Saturday taking one to tennis, one to swimming and the other to football and then sitting in the car for hours waiting for them to collect them at different times, getaway from Sunday mowing the parks and garden sized yard she had insisted I make as Saturday was overwhelmed by events that any loving Dad must do, why not pay for the parks and gardens to be done, you may ask.

"Two reasons, firstly you get abused up hill and down dale for being a lazy bastard and wasting money we supposedly don't have, I must have been away when the kids were eating bread and dripping like we had to do when we were young on occasions when money was tight, and we didn't have a decent pair of shoes for school.

"The other good and solid reason is you don't have to talk to her with the Victa at full throttle, I even used to mow the foot paths to stretch it out and then there was going to the local service station on the pretext of topping up the fuel can. This gave me a chance to talk on sensible subjects with the throngs of other parks and garden Dads who also were getting away and all being very kind, letting you first in the line as they hung back pretending to examine the oil cans in the garage rack. I'm in no rush, they would say and why would they be.

"So, my thoughts about long marriage is the getaway plan. That's the answer, saved my sanity and marriage. I was content to be locked up with 70 or so other blokes leading a mundane life in a big tin can, but safe and contented in our structured days. Outside of our working hours, all we had to worry about was when they were going to tie the black sewer pipe (submarine) up somewhere so we could go and play up for the few days we had alongside?

I never did the naughty bits but gave the booze a nudge occasionally. I was not that lucky with the ladies but also as Coxswain (chief of the boat), I was expected to behave myself. Not a good look for the Coxswain to be on stoppage of leave for CDA (caught disease ashore)"

"So, my old friend. Perhaps it's because we disobeyed all the husband rules that we have kept the wives interested and still hopeful that they can mold us into the ideal husbands according to their specifications and guidelines"

Raucous laughter filled the car,

"Well done Tezzay well done". says Lofty

"No, well done us. It's been years since we've had a full-on bullshit session. You haven't lost the magic of storytelling Tezza. I half believed all that crap you unloaded until I realised it was you doing your usual wind up" says lofty

"One thing has a bit of truth for both of us, I think. we both spent a lot of time away from the homestead and all the responsibilities that go with it, and mate I bloody well loved it and I think you did to" says Tezza

"I hope the wives never get hold of this conversation, I can't afford a divorce," says Lofty smiling at the thoughts Tezza had espoused

"don't worry mate my lips are sealed"

"Speaking of lips. Gawd I'm hungry mate, let's get some food" says Lofty.

THE McSTODGE INCIDENT

They left very early in the day and the cup of tea and the green stuff that Tezza insisted on feeding him was not sufficient to sustain Loftys portly figure.

As the highway bypassed many small towns it's not easy to find a good greasy spoon restaurant of the type Lofty loved. Lofty's thoughts turned to a McStodge brekky in the service centre a few Kms down the road.

"How about we stop at the next McStodge for some Brekky Tezza??"

A look of astonishment was Tezza's reply. "Well," said Lofty. Tezza's reply was not unexpected considering his stealthier figure and love of sports.

" Mate, I wouldn't feed that shit to a dog!!"

Taken aback Lofty suggests just a quick cup of coffee perhaps. It's clear that Tezza is not going to bend but the coffee suggestion seemed to be the middle ground.

"OK but I'm not going in there to get it, OK. I'm a bit tired from lack of sleep thanks to that horrible bed thing you put me on last night

"OK, I'll go, you put your seat back and get some rest. Remember you're driving this thing a bit further up the road and I don't want to wind up in a tree like we did on our way to Canberra" says Lofty

A sideways look and a cheeky grin reveals that Tezza remembers that little sidetrack and recalls it was all part of a shortcut that went wrong. Bloody Lofty, he's never going to let that one drop. How does he remember all this stuff, I can barely remember what I had for Brekky.

As the friendly banter continues and Lofty explains and apologises for the uncomfortable bed thing, the first of the warning signs (as Tezza puts it) comes into view. 5km to MSG the weathered sign says. The fast-food chain had been trying to play down the logo for years but the McStodge Group were stuck with it now.

The unfortunate name was based on the company's founder Malcolm Stephen McStodge, hence the MSG signs erected all over the place despite advice to the contrary from the marketing guys. The name stuck and the food unfortunately reflected the sign. The

MSG logo had become a tradition for quick and cheap fast food that was particularly enjoyable to Lofty who was known to eat almost anything.

It wasn't long before the big MSG sign loomed large in the windscreen as Tezza's protests increased

"You're not eating that shit Lofty. Just pull over near a rubbish bin and I'll find you with something better, said Tezza.

Ignoring the commentary Lofty lays down the law as he navigates his way into the parking lot.

"You just wait here in the car old fella, and I'll get some stuff and bring you a coffee, then we can pull over down the road somewhere and find you some grass for you to graze on OK!"

Tezza curls up under his hat, muttering about bringing him a flat white, no sugar.

Pulling into the parking area it was clear that the previous night had been a big one at MSG. Lofty finds himself a remote parking space. Making his way to the front door and avoiding the pile of regurgitated something, overflowing bins and a car full of sleeping drunks in various states of dress and undress. Loud music greets him from a panel van parked in the disabled spot where a couple of tradies have stopped for breakfast, a pair of dirty thong clad feet hanging out the passenger's side window marks the ambience of the place.

The entry was a little greasy as Lofty gingerly made his way inside. Looking down to avoid treading in something unpleasant a loud voice penetrates his concentration. EXCUSE ME!!! A large female in stretch pants pushes past to fulfill her fast-food mission of some sort and catch up with 2 little ferals who were busy pulling crap out of the bins.

"Get out the fucking bins ya little shits" Yells the muffin topped female "

How many fuckin times I gotta tell ya there's no bloody trading cards in the bloody bins" WHACK, WHACK and both kids are lifted off the bin and hurled towards the front door with the precision of a snooker champion.

Lofty's amusement at the scene is interrupted as he enters the noisy restaurant. From behind an electronic board, he is startled when a head appears around the corner of the board. With a toothy grin, an ageing female body appears and says

"Have you had a nice day sir and welcome to Stodges, blah blah blah." Meanwhile, the line is growing at the counter.

Thinking it must be a local deranged consumers suffering from mad cow disease or something, but the MSG badge pinned to the brown and yellow uniform is confirms she is an employee. The badge reads Miss Turd Hostess. It looks like some wag had blanked out some of the letters with white out.

Lofty being lofty responds with the following,

"What bloody day, madam its 7am in the morning"

Not fazed by the curt response the elderly school Maam type hostess continues her spiel explianing the electronic menu board's purpose as a bunch of school kids and a couple of tradies head past to further congest the counter area.

"Thanks, but I'm only after a McStodge breakfast and a coffee" says Lofty.

Not to be put off her spiel Miss Turd stops Lofty leaving by holding his arm

"But sir you can order"

Her voice trailing after him as Lofty breaks free and makes his way to join the lengthening queue at the counter.

Trying to stay in the queue and keep out of the way Lofty notices the two little bin diving darlings from saw earlier heading his way at 100mph with a trays full of stuff.

Before he could move, the contents of a containers full of white goo is tipped down the front of his shorts and over his shoes. The female Mountain of a mother arrives and begins chastising Lofty for tripping her little darlings over. Hostess, Miss Turd promptly arrives and gives a lecture on manners and behavior to Lofty.

At that moment, a bus load of Asian tourists arrives and heads to the spot Lofty had occupied before the little darlings covered him with the white stuff. Hostess lady apologizing profusely gives the fat mother a voucher and toys in a plastic bag and leaves.

Covered in crap and now at the back of a very long queue of non-English speaking Muppets with no idea of what they want or even know why they are on some strange cultural experience part of their tour, Lofty looks destined for a long wait.

Meanwhile with the sound of loud music blaring and Chinese selfies being taken a fracas has broken out in the drive through with a cup full of something flying through the window and hitting one of the kids trying to serve the Asian tourists through their interpreter with some difficulty.

The overall scene was rapidly descending into chaos. A pensioner on a walking frame had lost his way and wandered into the kitchen upsetting a tray of buns. A family was trying to escape the chaos to continue their holiday despite being detained by Miss Turd handing out come again pamphlets.

Loud music was blaring to the extent that the counter staff were having trouble hearing and orders were being misread and delivered causing more disruption. Behind the counter bells keep ringing somewhere deep in the bowels of the kitchen. A kid serving at the counter throws his hands in the air and tosses his apron and pointy hat on the counter,

"that's it, stick your job up your arse, I'm out of here"

Lofty is beginning to get a bad feeling about this as now there is only one young girl on the counter serving a growing line of customers. Meanwhile, chaos has erupted at the drive through with a buxom MSG person now reaching out of her window and slapping the disgruntled driver whilst his passenger climbs over the bonnet and trys to rip her headphones off her head.

A couple of tradies behind the offending car have started fighting with the other passengers in the offending care. Hostess, Miss Turd, is screaming

"Call the police, call the police"

Meanwhile, the Asian tourists are hustled out the door slipping and sliding on the white goo and other crap on the entrance way with Hostess person apologising and bowing as they leave the place.

With the drive through fight over and the counter under control again, Lofty finally makes it to the order area. The McStodge girl covered in food smiles timidly and takes Lofty's order. Deciding to use the waiting time efficiently, Lofty grabs a load of napkins to clean off the white goo.

After an anxious 20-minute wait and order numbers being called, the place is beginning to empty. Heading to the counter concerned his order had been missed politely asks the harassed young girl what has happened.

"Please wait your turn sir" says the counter person with a couple of fries stuck in her hair and mustard down her cheek.

Trying to explain Lofty finds the toothy geriatric Hostess Miss Turd beside him again.

"Oh!! It's you again, If you keep making trouble sir you will have to leave" she says "

Rising to his full height and ignoring Miss Turd, Lofty reaches over the counter with his ticket and let's fly.

"Listen, you little shit, I've been here for over 20 minutes. I'm covered in white goo from some feral kids; I've been abused by this idiot Hostess of yours and

IM FUCKING HUNGRY AND WANT MY FOOD NOW!!"

The counter person gingerly takes the ticket from Lofty whilst Hostess person goes in search of the manager who is attending to a skirmish in the car park.

A few minutes later the counter person returns with a bag full of stuff and the coffee apologising saying

"We are sorry sir we thought you had left when the fight broke out."

Seeing the distressed look in the young girl's eyes, Lofty has a moment of remorse.

"No worries love, Im sorry I yelled and swore at you, it's been a difficult day for you guys hasn't it"

The wistful smile on the girl's face said it all as Lofty turns to head out the door. He hadnt got far when he was confronted by the manager heading back into the restaurant with Miss Turd bending his ear. The disheveled manager with a black eye and crap all down his front stops Lofty on his way out whilst Miss Turd folds her arms smugly.

Lofty is not a small man even though age has weathered him. The twenty-something manager came up to his chest and seemed overwhelmed by the whole situation as drips of thick shake run down his face.

"Sir, we've had a complaint about your behaviour"

Cutting him off mid-sentence and leaning close to the manager's ear Lofty says

"If you don't get out of my way right now, I'm going to put you and Miss Turd in that rubbish bin over there"

The manager seems to get the message and judging by his state of dress and black eye might have had enough aggravation for one day and departs with Miss Turd bending his ear as they go.

Lofty slips and slides his way out the door to the car park being careful not to spill Tezza's coffee in the cheap paper cup. Arriving at the car he finds Tezza asleep and a large pickup truck parked close to his driver's door. With great care he manages to open the driver's side door but, in the process, drops the coffee cup and the bag of McStodge which with all the delays has gone cold and the flimsy recyclable bag failing with grease seeping through it.

"Ahhh! Fuckit" exclaims Lofty, climbing into the driver's seat and rousing Tezza who asks,

"So, where's my coffee?

"Don't ask" says Lofty slipping the car into reverse.

The reversing proximity alarm sounds and glancing at the rear-view mirror Lofty sees a short plump man in a hi visibility vest holding up his hand for them to stop.

"What now," says Lofty?

The little man appears at the window and demands an explanation as to why Lofty was littering his car park and demanding he picks it up. Meanwhile, the fat lady with the feral kids is stuck behind Lofty and Tezza's car and honking her horn to get past having made a second sortie to the drive through with her gift card from Miss Turd.

"That's it," says Lofty jumping out of the car, scooping up the mess he heads over to the fat lady's car and taps on the window.

"Madam, I'm sure you missed out on the McStodge special breakfast this morning so here take mine"

Thrusting the mess in through the window and storming back to the car he stops at the little fat man in the hi visibility vest and says

"OK, Happy now, I've put the rubbish where it belongs so get out of the way unless you want to become a permanent part of my car"

Gingerly the little fat man steps aside as Lofty climbs back into the car and floors it and leaving a trail of tyre smoke and spraying refuse and crap all over the little fat man and the feral ladies car.

"So old mate what was that all about," says Tezza.

"Don't ask just point me to the nearest servo so I can clean up and get something to eat" says Lofty.

A short time later the pair finds a truck stop. Lofty avails himself of the showers while Tezza orders a breakfast of bacon and eggs and coffee for them both. Back on the road again, and feeling refreshed, the pair walked out into the mid-morning sun. Explaining that he needs to get some sleep after all the excitement at McStodges, Lofty climbs into the passenger seat and curls up for some shut eye.

Getting behind the wheel Tezza says,

"Whats wrong old mate. I know how you love driving and weve not been on the road for long and you have got me driving already, what's the score??"

Pulling his cap down over his eyes Lofty is clearly grumpy

"Just drive the bloody car OK"

NAVAL DAZE

Tezza doesn't usually let his mind wonder back to their Navy days but he is certainly guilty of using phrases and expressions from that era from his past life and long service in the Navy. After swerving to miss a bit of roadkill and almost becoming a bonnet mascot on a semi-trailer rig, the violent maneuvers have woken Lofty with start,

What the hell was that all about. Maybe I should take over the driving again before you get us both killed"

Tezza now had Lofty's wide-eyed full attention.

"Tezza you are now on the wrong side of your twilight years and you still can't bloody drive"

Slightly annoyed Tezza responds to now wide-awake Lofty glaring at him from the passenger's seat.

"If you bring up that bloody incident in the old car back in 65 again, I swear I will pull up at the next McStodge order double and make you eat it. If you recall it was my driving skills during that incident that allowed us to be here today." He says with a small amount of venom in his voice.

"Yeh yeh Tezza I have heard your version before but believe me you silly old fool your version is best remembered during a long drinking session."

"So now you're questioning my memory. Let's see if you can remember a few little instances when I saved you scrawny neck at your old favourite eatery."

SQUEEZE GUTS AND PNEUMONIA BRIDGE

The story rolled out about a time in UK when the pair had just left a greasy spoon cafe whose cuisine would not be allowed in a refugee camp or prison and Lofty's attempt to eat it like it was the winning entry in a My Kitchen Rules final.

"youre talking about Squeeze Guts Café aren't you" asks Lofty

"Spot on. The tucker from there was probably no worse than any other dump at the time but, we ate there because we were usually out of it from drinking skrumpy (thick cider) and you were into the Squeeze gut tucker like a hungry lion. You will then remember walking back to our accommodation you spilled your guts all over Pneumonia Bridge."

No, can't remember that but it was the norm after one of Squeeze guts delicacies" says Lofty faking a stomach heave

"Okay, lets reconstruct the scene, its pitch black and we are crossing a steep bridge that I am sure was built by the Romans and it is colder than a look from the missus after pay day, or maybe it was because I was dodging carrots and scrumpy as well as other things that you had eaten and were regurgitating, not because of the tucker from squeeze guts but because you were a lousy drunk I reckon and if it wasn't for me you would have been certain to have fallen off that rotten old bridge and into the mud and slime below, so you owe me one" .says Tezza

"You sure it wasn't the other way round Tezza" says Lofty grinning.

The banter and stories continue for a while as the duo heads down the highway reliving their youthful days and exploits and giggling like a pair of naughty schoolboys from time to time.

SUBMARINERS CUISINE

With a doubtful frown on his face, Tezza reverts the discussion back to food so they could finish their previous conversation. They both agreed that their constitutions for drinking had been hardened up due to their exploits as 20-year-old submariners in the UK, they agreed that their stomachs were prepared for the future wives cooking during the same period.

From there it was all downhill with them both recalling the delights of things like a doughy, bready pie with tinned sausages standing upright presumably ready to salute any brave soul dopey enough to be first to dig in. Then there was a little dish called Toad in the Hole, on a scale of 10 it earns a generous 2.5, a repast certainly not fit for pigs. But they always went back for seconds

They went on to recall other submarine delicacies like some form of suet, gravy, and some horrible indescribable meat with the horrible name of Babies Heads and so it went on as the pair drove on into the day making themselves sick at the thought of some of the recipes.

They agreed that those were interesting times and despite everything they loved them and every piece of the puzzle, good or bad was one unbelievable adventure and a memorable time in their lives.

"I think I will concentrate on the road for a while and you can shut your eyes and dream of your world and leave the real one to me for the time being. Just to help you relax, forget about the car accident I saved you from" say Tezza

Having given Tezza the royal finger salute, Lofty settles back in his seat, pulls his hat down over his eyes and nods off back to sleep

The car rumbles along the freeway and through the glorious scenery as Lofty dozed in the passenger seat. Time passes uneventfully when a bump in the never-ending road work wakes Lofty from his dreams.

"Thank God for that, I don't think I could stand that bloody snoring any longer let alone it is coming from both ends. I'm sure something's died up there. I've had to drive with the window down". says Tezza

"You're always complaining. Just hit the climate control and set the fan to extract here see" says Lofty pushing buttons and explaining how his Missus does it all the time.

"What, she farts a lot" says Tezza.

"Yeh that too but she's good at pushing buttons."

"Aren't they all, said Tezza.

"Too true, too true, anyway mate, it's me you're talking to remember, I'm bloody useless at this hi-tech stuff". Says Tezza

Having got the memories out of the way they had planned for a lunch stop at a favourite eatery of Lofties. The eating hole they were heading for had a place in Lofty's heart. As part of his last job, he often came up this way and would eat there and sometimes stay overnight. The Gumnut Café, situated right in the middle of a beautiful town with fantastic food according to Lofty. Tezza, although doubtful agreed to give it a go even though Lofty's lpast choices of eaterys left doubts about his choices.

This time however, Loftys choice was spot on and the pair enjoyed a hearty late lunch and a stroll around the little town picking up some snacks for the road. It had been a tiring first day with the early start and incidents along the way had worn them out so the decision to find a comfortable motel for the night seemed the right thing to do.

A COUPLE OF GAYS

The two intrepid travelers drove until a motel took their fancy about 6pm. They were in no rush and weren't constrained by any time frame except that set by their wives who were no doubt enjoying themselves anyway.

The motel proprietor greeted them with a friendly smile, and announced that he was sorry but couldn't offer them separate rooms as the motel was full of mining workers

"No problem that suits us as single room will do, says Tezza realising they were both too tired to go further,

The desk clerk, thinking he must have seen something between the travelers that really wasn't there, explained that the room only had two single beds but they could get them pushed together if needs be.

Lofty jumped in quickly, faking a rather gay voice,

"That will be fine sweety, we are not a couple yet, but who knows. Can you direct my man here to a good place for dinner sweety." He said as he minced back to the car leaving Tezza horrified and making all sorts of excuses that weren't working with the desk clerk. Tezza was not tolerant towards men who preferred men and certainly did not take kindly to be thought of as one,

Once established in their room, the guys debated whether to shower now or later, the latter won and they decided a good stroll before dinner would suit them both after a long day sitting in the car.

Glaring at Lofty Tezza gives him a piece of his mind.

"Thanks for embarrassing me with that performance at the desk."

"That's OK, I rang him back later when you were outside and asked him over for a threesome. says Lofty

The look on Tezza's face said it all.

"Only joking mate but got you going there didn't I."

They walked for 15 minutes before it became obvious that Lofty was exhausted and slowing down. His weight challenged body contributed to there pace as they slowed their walk until they found the restaurant that the motel proprietor had recommended and sat down to eat.

True to expectations Lofty put the waitress's fitness to the test as she did more than a few laps from their table to the kitchen, Tezza did not want to spoil the congenial atmosphere and did not remind Lofty of his earlier weight affected walk and that they still had to walk back to the motel.

They were into their second beer and they decided to forego the coffee. A discussion on beers they had dunk in their youth filled in the rest of the evening until it was time to go back to the Motel.

Walking slowly the pair recalled many drunken nights and fun they had in their youth

"It says something about our mentality at that age doesn't it", says Tezza

"It sure does, no wonder we are brain dead now, but by God, wouldn't we do it all over again". says Lofty

"Speaking of getting shit faced it was difficult at times to work out the difference between sober and drunk, by that I mean we were shit faced as a given and occasionally got sober, those were the days mate," says Tezza as they strolled along recalling their mis spent youth.

BALCONY EXCURSIONS

After a restless night and Lofty's snoring Tezza was feeling a little jaded and noticed there was a daily Yoga class in the courtyard below their room that might refresh him for the day ahead if followed by a swim in the pool.

The courtyard was busy with mostly ladies setting out their yoga mats and it appeared as though Tezza was the only male to join the group with his towel as a mat.

A 40 something lady in skintight yoga gear sauntered over and introduced herself as the hotel owner's wife offering Tezza a spare mat to put on the grass.

"Good morning, you must be one of the gay guys in No5" she said bending over in front of Tezza without and concern for the appealing view he had of her rear end Tezza was enjoying.

Before he could answer she winked at him saying.

"Its fine sweety, pity though" she says with knowing wink. Tezza thinks this gay thing might be the road to letting females convert him.

The yoga session commenced and the instructor's voice woke Lofty up. Looking down from the balcony Lofty could see Tezza amongst the females doing his exercises and thinking, I don't know how he does it, meaning Tezza might pull a bird before breakfast.

Enjoying the scene of women bending and stretching Lofty had the urge to fart. Undoubtably a result of last night's indulgences, he let fly a very loud fart that surprised him as well as the assembled exercise class below.

"Sorry" was all he could think of to say as the sound echoed around the courtyard.

After a look of disgust from the assembled exercisers a voice rang out agross the courtyard from a nearby balcony.

"Call that a fart" a large man in high visibility shirt and underpants let fly a long and loud fart smiling across at Lofty

"Your full of shit, no skill" calls another voice from a distant balcony as he let fly with a trumpeting fart that would have woken the dead. Not to be out done farter number one lets go another loud fart.

"Cop that you underground rat" he says with a champions salute

Other voices chime it with points as a third man enters the contest and a cacophony of farts echo around the small courtyard.

The Yogo ladies decide to pack up whilst Tezza glares up at Lofty with his arms raised.

Later when he returned to the room Tezza let Lofty know he had ruined a likely intimate encounter and probably cemented their reputation as the farting gays, they had better get out before we get a cleaning bill for the courtyard.

Making a hasty pack up and exit the pair hit the road and individually giggle as they thought about the farting contest and ate the remains of their room service breakfast.

AGEING
DISGRACEFULLY

B ack on the road again they looked at the moonscape that was once beautiful fields and paddocks but was now open cut mine sites as far as the eye could see.

"Well, it is good to be on the road again and in all honesty, I don't feel too bad" says Lofty.

"No but you sure do smell bad ole son, what on earth did you eat last night" says Tezza opening the driver side window.

Ignoring Tezza's protests Lofty continues his train of thought.

"I thought I would be crook after last night's session when I woke up this morning. I was not sure I could take big night out.

However, I've changed my mind; I am now looking forward to round two" says Lofty.

INNOVATION AND TECHNOLOGY

As the trip rolls on and thoughts turn to other things Tezza puts his dislike of technology, forward.

"I was thinking about how much of a status symbol mobile phones have become. Seems like everyone has one these things glued their hands or stuck on their ears these days mate, says Tezza making signs of dialling on a phone.

My 85-year-old cousin says he can't afford one, so he's wearing his garage door opener. Now everyone thinks that he's cool, or off his brain or both. The thought brings forth a round of laughter and sympathy from the traveling pair.

"Anyway while you were snoring, says Tezza, I was thinking about a few things and how we could contribute to our age group. Like for instance:

How about putting pictures of missing husbands on beer cans The laughter starts again and it was clear that each would now take it in turns to add to the list as they carried on down the road

"I was thinking about defining old age and decided that it is when you still have something on the ball but you are just too tired to bounce it. says Tezza slumping forward

More laughter and a side comment about Balls in general and their diminishing use.

"Lofty, you know I like to go to the gym, " explains Tezza

"I thought about making a fitness movie for folks our age and call it, 'Pumping Rust'. It was clear this ludicrous list was not going to end there and the banter came thick and fast

"Lofty I have got that dreaded furniture disease, with a sorrowful look on his face, that's when your chest is falling into my drawers!"

"Tezza, you know when people visit and see a cat's litter box, they always say, "Oh, have you got a cat?" Just once I wanted to say, "No, it's for visitors to use, do you need to go?!"

Tezza picks up the thread,

"Employment application blanks always ask who is to be notified in case of an emergency. I think you should write, "A Good Doctor!"

"Makes sense to me" says Lofty,

"Tell me, why do they put posters of wanted criminals up in Post Offices? What are we supposed to do, write to them?

Why don't they just put their pictures on postage stamps so the posties could keep an eye out while they delivered the mail?"

"Tezza, my son is fascinated with cleaning? Does a clean house indicate that there is a broken computer in it?"

"Can't answer that mate but why is it that no matter what colour of bubble bath you use, the bubbles are always white?

"You got me there Tezza but answer me this. Why do our sons and daughters constantly return to the refrigerator with the hopes that something new to eat will have materialized?"

"That sounds more like you ole son," said Tezza.

"Piss off Tezza, just because I like to eat"

Before Lofty can finish his sentence Tezza chips in.

"Ok, calm down. Tell me why women keep running over a string a dozen times with their vacuum cleaner, then reach down, pick it up, examine it, then put it down to give their vacuum one more chance?"

"Now you're onto something. I think it's a wife thing, for instance, my missus can't work out why no plastic garbage bag will open from the end she first tries and can't tell the difference between a yard sale and a trash pickup."

"I've told her it depends on how close to the road the stuff is placed?"

"Yep, I know what you mean mate. Can't figure mine out either. For example, in winter, why does she keep the house as warm as it was in summer when she complains about the heat in summer??"

Lofty responds, "Mate, I guess it comes down to that old motto. If at first you don't succeed, shouldn't you try doing it like your wife told you to?

Tezza ole mate, I know you've got religious leanings so can you explain why old folks seem to read the Bible a whole lot more as they get older."

Tezza responds with a glint in his eye.

"That's easy, you heathen bastard. They're cramming for their finals. As for me, I'm just hoping the man upstairs grades me on a curve rather than pass/fail."

The car rocks with laughter as the pair decide that it was the end of that little diversion into insanity. The car motors on through the countryside as the thought of a lunch stop crosses Lofties mind.

Breaking the silence Lofty puts forward a plan "As we discussed at breakfast, there's a great place about 50kms up the road from here according to this map. I've been there before and trust me the food is good and don't tell me you're not hungry." Tezza's nod of agreement seals the decision as the discussion descends into Lofty's motor biking days.

Looking across at Lofty, Tezza decides its joke time.

"Okay Mr amusement to fill in the time to lunch we should have a little joke contest" says Tezza remembering one he heard some time back thats a sure winner

JOKE TIME

THE WALRUS

"Here my first offering" says Tezza

Picture its, summer in the Antarctic and it is hot, global warming and all that crap. A yound female Walrus is driving along when steam pisses out from under the bonnet of her sealmobile, she pulls into a garage and a big polar bear comes out,

I'll look at for you he says, explaining that she can go down the road to the ice cream shop and get an ice cream to cool off and when she comes back he should have an answer to the problem with the seal mobile

Lofty interjects, wait a minute chief, heatwave in Antartica, polar bears dont live down there, icream shop? this sounds like something the government might suggest.

Looking annoyed Tezza cuts in, Ok Ok I know its a farse remember so stop running my joke or I will take points off yours OK!

Continuing with the joke:

So off she goes buys herself a vanilla ice cream, (thats the only flavour they have down there) and although she doesn't notice because she is a messy eater and it's a hot day, the ice cream melts and is all over her mouth.

Hold it again chief. why only one flavour and you forgot to note her big Walrus teeth, says Lofty

Shut up and let me finish this now ruined joke before I forget the punchline says Tezza

So lady Walrus approaches the polar bear who says to her, you have blown a seal, completely embarrassed she replies, oh no its ice cream really.

"Five out of ten a bloody shocker." says Lofty smiling,

"Yer right Ronnie Corbett, Jack Benny or whoever you modeled yourself off, your turn." Says Tezza

"Not much to beat "says, Lofty.

THE ELEPHANTS EAR

This bloke goes into a classy joint, at least 2 above a takeaway. The waiter approaches but doesn't have a menu, the bloke says where's the menu, don't need one says the waiter, we pride ourselves that we can deliver anything that the customer orders and if we don't his second choice plus wine are free. The bloke thinks to himself here's a free steak and wine coming up, I'll have an elephant's ear on a roll thank you, the waiter doesn't flinch, will that be an Indian or African elephant sir, I'll give you a little leeway says the bloke and smugly, either will do,

Thank you sir and off he goes. A few minutes later he comes back looking very sheepish,

Got you said the customer no elephant ears? No, said the waiter no rolls.

"Pathetic, even worse than mine, I am not even going to score it, Billy Connelly you're not." Says Tezza

Laughing quietly to themselves, neither Tezza nor Lofty could think of anything that would outdo the other so both sat back to enjoy a bit of quiet and looked forward to the next stop.

HANDS TO BATH

Having stopped for quick lunch and with Tezza driving Lofty points to a lovely golden beach and they decide its time for a dip. Heading into a car park beside a long beach Lofty says.

"Pull up over there near the beach. I really need a wash and a swim"

"Sounds like a good idea mate, I'm up for that" says Tezza. After some discussion regarding the location and lack of appropriate beach attire it was decided that a swim in their underpants would be fine. The intrepid bathers set off down to the water in their poorly fitting undies.

After a half hour of enjoying the water and splashing about like a pair of kids the two old vets head back up to the car to dry off. The carpark had filled up whilst they were away and the sight of the two old men in wet, see through badly fitting undies sparked a round of laughter and disgust as mothers covered their young children's eyes.

Oblivious to all this the men walked proudly to their car and dried themselves off with the towels they had pinched from the motel. A tap on the shoulder by a rather large lifeguard startled Tezza.

"Gents, nude bathing is not permitted here, this is a family beach so I'm going to ask you both to leave," said the lifeguard

"No worries, Chief we are on our way anyway" says Tezza as his towel drops revealing his naked nether regions

"Right, that's it your both going to be detained for indecent exposure, Says the lifeguard draping the towel around Tezza.

On the driver's side Lofty noted the discussions and jumped in the driver's seat and started the car. With a quick move Tezza avoids the lifeguard and jumps in the passenger's seat as Lofty backs the car out with tyres squealing and the lifeguard hanging off the side mirror.

Tezza lowers the window and apologises.

"Sorry mate, we've got to get back to the asylum" as he winds the window up.

A crunch behind the car startled Lofty but he plants his foot as Tezza looks behind to see what they hit.

"Mate, you just did a good deed for humanity": he says

Noting the lifeguard had given up pursuit. Lofty looks across at Tezza smiling.

"So, what did I hit and should I stop?" he says

"No mate you just ran over a climate change protest booth and knocked over a big picture of Greta Thundberg. Best we get well away from here and maybe change cars at the next major town just in case"

After taking advantage of a long drop dunny the lads swap places with Lofty taking the wheel, they head back to the unending highway via some back roads that Lofty knew of to avoid any police scrutiny.

Settling back into the drive Lofty ponders the event at the beach.

"What happened back there seemed normal to me but I wonder if it's because we are getting older or just more stupid. I have a theory about what happens to our brain as we age."

Oh god here we go again, but ok I'm a bit bored so entertain me with your theory" says Tezza.

"Hear me out I think there's something in this for us both" says Lofty

With his eyes rolled up Tezza motions with his hands.

"Lead on professor Lofty"

THE 20% MAN

"For, those of us, who are still young at heart whilst the rest of the body has gone south, will understand all about 20% Man (or woman).

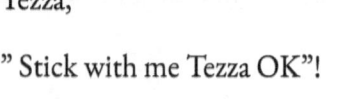

"OK, you've got me there what's that have to do with our beach debacle" says Tezza,

" Stick with me Tezza OK"!

"20% man is that part of you that got you into trouble in the first place. You remember the shit we did when we were in our teens and 20's??"

"Yes, but I'm trying to forget that stuff Lofty" says Tezza.

Lofty explains, 20% man the one who has the extra bourbon, pushes the throttle a little harder, does silly dance steps and ogles young girls at the beach or on yoga mats. He was largely responsible for what happened to you between 18 and 30 years old.

"Mate, I'm still doing some of that stuff "says Tezza laughing!

"That's the point old friend." Lofty goes on to explain.

"80% man is the normal self, and you know him well at our age. He controls most of your day-to-day stuff, puts on the suit at weddings and funerals and smiles at the mother-in-law whilst making small talk with boring relatives. He knows 20% man well and does his best to suppress him whenever he appears.

Tezza nodding in agreement says,

"So, your theory is that as we age, we need to keep 20% man under control to avoid killing ourselves."

"Absolutely there is, of course, another control factor that most of us mere males are aware of says, Lofty says glancing knowledgeably sideways at Tezza.

"What's some sort of mind control I always thought you were a bit of pot smoking hippy". says Tezza,

Lofty's raised hand stops Tezza in mid-sentence.

"No, it's simpler than all of that. It's known as the leader of the opposition, the boss, her indoors and the little lady, in more patronizing terms. This form of control over 20% man works occasionally but he is generally deaf to female voices. says Lofty continuing his lecture

"80% man, however, is very much aware of the penalties for ignoring the female control factor. In fact, he has developed a wonderful unambiguous response called the 'Yes Dear' response. I've made a career out of controlling 20% man with varying levels of success with that phrase" says Lofty.

"OK I'm on the same wavelength now, that's a good theory but how about some examples? Says Tezza

"Right, take our beach romp, who oversaw our brains then? says Lofty.

Before he could answer lofty cuts in.

"20% man of course. No female control through 80% man there. Then as we took off it would not have been an 80%-man decision would it." says Lofty

"Okay, I think you have something but please let 80% man do the driving."

The journey continues with Lofty wondering if they might drop in and see Davidio's (Dave to his friends) new place. Agreeing with the proposition they decide to give Dave a call.

"Give him a call Tezza. Just push the screen button and select phone then scroll down to contacts.........Cutting across Lofty's instructions Tezza says

"Mate, this is me you're talking to. I have trouble with the garage door opener let alone all this stuff. Which reminds me, wasn't life supposed to get easier when we retired and isn't all this technological stuff supposed to be simple enough for a ten-year-old to operate."

"Tezza, we haven't got a ten-year-old and I'm not stopping to find one so let's just call him when we stop next. You know I need a pee every 100kms or so anyway so it won't be long." Says Lofty.

"Yes, but I would prefer it if you stopped and got out of the car first, it's beginning to stink in here". says Tezza

"Mate, that's your incontinence pads that have gone off not mine" replies Lofty.

More laughter ensues. And finally after a quick roadside pee stop, contact with Dave is made and arrival instructions were received.

"It will be good to see Dave again. I think his retirement gulag looks pretty good on paper" says Tezza

"Yep, I hope we don't upset his missus as she is not our biggest fan": says Lofty

"Should be ok, I think she is supposed to be away anyhow so if we behave we should be fine", says Tezza

"Behave, us, behave," says Lofty and the pair laugh as they continue down the road.

Looking at the beautiful, picture postcard scenery as it flashes by the car windows Lofty is prompted to speak

"How would you like to wake up to that every morning? It's so serene, those oxygen thieves in Hippyville are maybe not so dumb after all, living off the taxpayers, no work, serenity and lots of free love and more." He says Tezza.

Yeh sounds good but not sure my free love ambitions would exceed my capabilities at this age and I would get kicked out as a non performer at the nightly orgy.

Both giggle as they conjure up thoughts of a hippy orgy in their minds.

THE NIGHT AT DAVE'S

P ulling into the driveway of a gated community in a rather opulent suburb Tezza feels obliged to comment.

Struth Lofty, you said the old sausage fingers (He with the short digits, so named....!) had done alright but this is much bloody better than just good.

Don't be fooled Tezza says Lofty, can't you see this is a detention centre for old farts, look at the gate and high fences. A bloke would never get over those with your knees and my back.

What are you talking about you old fool, says Tezza pointing at the elegant sign which read Earls Gate, and had 5 stars under it, this is an up market over 55's gated community.

Nah, says Lofty, that's just to fool the bleeding hearts and the greenies. See, says lofty pointing to an elderly couple wearing matching tracksuit with a little dog on a leash entering the side gate.

That lot is wearing prison overalls and has been out on day release and is bringing their dinner home on a leash.

You just don't know when to stop Lofty do you, says Tezza, talk about politically incorrect.

Just push the bell and get the warden to let us in Tezza, I'm getting hungry again.

Your always bloody hungry says Tezza reaching out to push the call button on the pedestal near the big gates.

The speaker crackles into life with Dave's voice.

We will have two medium meal deals and two large cokes please. Says Tezza into the speaker.

Smart arse says Dave. Just get your arse in here and park up under the trees around the side and make it snappy.

The speaker goes dead and big gates open majestically.Pulling into the driveway of a gated community in a rather opulent suburb Tezza feels obliged to comment.

Struth Lofty, you said the old sausage fingers (He with the short digits, so named....!) had done alright but this is much bloody better than just good.

Don't be fooled Tezza says Lofty, can't you see this is a detention centre for old farts, look at the gate and high fences. A bloke would never get over those with your knees and my back.

What are you talking about you old fool, says Tezza pointing at the elegant sign which read Earls Gate, and had 5 stars under it, this is an up market over 55's gated community.

Nah, says Lofty, that's just to fool the bleeding hearts and the greenies. See, says lofty pointing to an elderly Asian couple wearing matching tracksuit with a little dog on a leash entering the side gate.

That lot is wearing prison overalls and has been out on day release and is bringing their dinner home on a leash.

You just don't know when to stop Lofty do you, says Tezza, talk about politically incorrect.

Just push the bell and get the warden to let us in Tezza, I'm getting hungry again.

Your always bloody hungry says Tezza reaching out to push the call button on the pedestal near the big gates.

The speaker crackles into life with Dave's voice.

We will have two medium meal deals and two large cokes please. Says Tezza into the speaker.

Smart arse says Dave. Just get your arse in here and park up under the trees around the side and make it snappy.

The speaker goes dead and big gates open majestically."I reckon he's still the same old Dave," say Lofty as the car wafts along manicured streets with neat homes and perfect gardens. I seem to remember he liked his comforts.

"Bloody oath says Tezza heading the car towards a clump of trees and bushes as instructed. He's the only UC (submarine sonar operator) that I ever saw wearing a smoking jacket in the control room or taking his own wine glass for a run ashore in France."

The door to the house opens with Dave urgently ushering the pair to park over near a big tree beside the house.

"What's that all about" says Lofty.

"I think we are about to find out" says Tezza pointing to a minibus that has pulled into the driveway and up outside the front door.

"Must be Dave's wine order arriving" says lofty.

"Don't be silly you know he would have that delivered by helicopter mate" says Tezza laughing.

It wasn't long before the mystery was solved as Dave's missus slips out and into the minibus and the bus load of cackling women departs.

"Looks like Dave's missus has gone for the night" says Tezza, pity, I rather liked his missus.

Dave meanwhile is waving for the lads to come over to the house. Without much ado the pair renews their acquaintance with their old mate and settle down to some heavy drinking in Dave's spacious back room.

It wasn't long before Dave explained that his missus was going to be away overnight and that he didn't want her to know the lads were coming for a session.

David, she had said, (she always called him David when she was cross) do you remember the last time you got together with those two old fools in our old house. Dave of course had acted innocent at that point. Let me remind you David, she had said.

The police were called because you managed to set fire to the back fence with your fire pit idea. Old Fred across the road never forgave you for letting Lofty put his annoying, stinky cat in the washing machine and dumping it on his doorstep with a sign which read, ding dong dell pussy's been in the well, who put him there, I did because I hate your fucking stinky cats, signed Lofty the pussy bandit.

Then there was the loud music and poor singing that went on at all hours of the day and night. The neighbours were well over Pink Floyd but the site of you three singing rude songs on the front lawn in your undies was the final straw.

But, oh no, that wasn't enough, you had to let Tezza do colours at 8am on a Sunday morning still in your undies and the three of you with stolen traffic cones for hats whilst using a tea towel on a stick for a flag.

You may recall we had to move house and it's taken me 3 years to get over all that and God knows what else you three did. The locals who found out about the incident still look at me with pity thinking I'm married to a lunatic, which of course I did.

So, David they are not coming here... right. I don't want to move again.

"That was the jist of her instructions," said Dave

"Sorry Dave we promise to behave this time" with a slight smile on his face. says Tezza,

Topping up the lads' glasses,

"Yeh right, just like we did on our way home from the UK." Dave says

"Did we play up, can't remember that" says Tezza with a smirk on his face and eyes raised?

"Okay you pair of pricks let me refresh your memories." Says Dave standing up as he recounts the events and begins a series of sweeping moves around the room as he explains.

"The trip home through West and South Africa comes to mind. How about the carry on in Gibraltar where the skipper and Navigator gave our UC1 (head sonar petty officer) and Johns (second Coxn) names when they were evicted from a night club and failed to pay the taxi driver.

"That was the funniest Captains table I've ever seen, but who was it who wanted to smuggle a Barbary ape on board but wound up getting the shit beaten out of him by the bloody thing" said Tezza

"Those things are stronger than they look guys" says Dave.

"Bullshit Dave, it was a baby one you grabbed but it was the mother that got stuck into you. Regardless, the local fuzz was not impressed as you managed to upset the whole pack and they turned on a bunch of tourists who ran for their lives with ape shit being thrown at them and you."

"Anyway," says Dave, trying hard to put that story away for good.

"How about Accra, Senegal. We could smell the place three hours before we tied up at the wharf. Immediately it was off to the bars, or the beach. The beach was great White sand, blue sea and surf, until the next day, one of the beach parties complained that he had caught crabs off the beach Oh, come on pull the other one!" says Dave

"I don't think I made it to the beach, Tezza. I think I was on the cultural exchange tour with TW Yatt looking at grass huts held together with cow shit. They smelled worse than a stoker's armpits. "Said Tezza topping up their glasses

"I must have been duty" says Lofty smiling.

With a look of frustration, Dave continues his crabs story.

"Off we trooped to the local hospital, where we were de-loused and given hospital type gowns to wear, you know the ones two ties at the back and your arse hangs out!" says Dave

They sound better than pusser (Navy) pajamas put on backwards so you could carry your toothbrush discreetly, through the control room in your bum crack eh Dave", says Lofty,

"No mate these were the real deal with the full finesse de breeze opening in the back end". says Dave frowning

"The hospital was like something out of the 'Papillon' (Dustin Hoffman and Steve McQueen movie) Stone walls and no windows, bare cot beds with threadbare mattresses, with a male medical orderly that looked like a cadaverous serial-killer" explained Dave

"Senegals answer to HMAS Penguin," says Tezza giggling.

"We were the only ones in the Ward and after three or four hours of farting contests and rude jokes about the seven-foot tall and outwardly gay male nurse, we were feeling very bored." Explained Dave making rude gestures

"Through the window, we could hear music and laughter, so we decided to investigate. Out the window we went across a dirty field and to a high fence and the sound of music and people enjoying themselves on the other side. With only minor difficulty, we helped one another over the fence and were confronted with about a hundred locals celebrating the death of one of their family.

"The noise stopped at the sight of three near-naked white blokes who must have looked like ghosts or something to them. After the initial shock from both sides and pulling the splinters out of our arses from crawling over the fence, we joined in the wake. Just before dawn, we jumped the fence and headed back to the ward and were in bed before the sun came up and the serial-killer nurse re-appeared."

"Dave, there's something missing here, what happened at the wake?"

"Well, there was a little bit of a kafuffle when one of the lads relieved himself into the local's moonshine brew urn thinking it was a dunny, certainly smelt like one to me, and another one of us mistook the widow for a potential leg over opportunity"

"So, you didn't do your famous bum dance Dave" says Lofty.

"Not that night that came later" explained Dave getting frustrated at the interruptions to his story

"The bars were good fun. Lots of music (called 'High Life'), and dancing with beautiful lithe black girls who all looked like Dianna Ross, until you took them home and they took their wigs off! We couldn't understand why they all put their keys in a large ashtray in the middle of the table. I found out to my regret if a key was picked up. You became Dianna's for the night! Why is it the best-looking keys belonged to the ugliest girls" says Tezza.

"Looks typical of your experience with key parties' mate," says Lofty with a smirk on his face.

Cutting him off at the pass, Tezza says,

"I can remember that I wound up with one lady that had a coconut husk hair wig dyed blond. It gave me the fright of my life in the morning when I sobered up.

"Because of the hair," says Dave,

"No, she put her false teeth on top of the wig on the bed post at the head of the bed. I thought I was being attacked by a rabid wolf hound when I awoke." says Tezza with actions to emphasise the incident

The three old friends burst into laughter and headed to the fridge for more beer. The story continues with Lofty leading the way

"Alright guys, do you remember Accra, Ghana. A bit more civilized than Senegal, and they spoke English, and not bloody French! The local girls were just as nice though, but they took forever to unwrap thanks to those bloody great wrap around things they all wore. Bit like Christmas when you got to the present though."

"Yeh but it was well worth the effort eh!" Says Tezza.

"Kinda like a box of chocolates mate, you never knew what you got until you unwrapped the package." Says Dave quoting Forest Gumps style of speaking

Dave continues the story.

"You may recall we were invited to a party at the combined (UK, Australia) High Commission Compound, hosted by the Australian High Commissioner, Richard something or other I think was his name. Someone told us it was a Barbeque, so we all turned up dressed in swimmers and thongs with towels on our arms (The compound had a swimming pool). Everyone else was dressed in evening wear!

"The High Commissioner had stocked the bar with unlimited large cans of Fosters and VB Beer, and the chef was flat out barbecuing a whole steer on an open pit. I got the impression we were in for a good night.

"The fun started when we became tempted by music and alcohol, to invite the female guests to have a swim in the pool, albeit an involuntary one! At least we also got to have a dip in the pool the next day, when we were back at the compound scouring the bottom of the pool for the lost jewelry. I didn't realize how difficult it would be to spot a diamond necklace on the bottom of a pristine swimming pool!" says Dave

"I must have been duty" says Lofty, smiling.

"It was the after-party fun that I recall eh Lofty". Says Tezza

"I must have been duty again" says Lofty again.

"Bullshit, you remember the local football club lined up some fun for us and you had your way with a local lovely but had no money. The cabby had to beat off the ladies so he could get paid instead of them." Says Tezza

"Oh, that incident. I must have been duty, can't remember that." Said Lofty

"You still owe me $20, tight wad" says Tezza.

"No worries, I'll get you a head job at the next aged care place we pass on the trip. However, I do recall you telling me about how they saved the condoms by washing them. Pretty full clothesline that day as I recall." say Lofty

"I must have been duty" says Tezza with a smirk.

The three old fools down their beers and the discussions descend into fruity details and much laughter. The evening was warm and pleasant so the three retired outside to Dave's grass hut style Bali room. Recovering from the mirth of Ghana and settling back in the cane chairs with another beer and some snorting port, Dave continues the travel log.

"Cape Town, South Africa, Remember that place" says Dave?

"Must have been duty" says Tezza...

Dave pushes on with his story.

"This city was an eye-opener for an Australian, as Apartheid was the rule of the day. The segregation of "Blancs" and "Non Blancs" even applied to park benches! On the bus from Simon's Town to Cape Town, the vehicle had a black line running across the inside, with: Non Blancs" forward in the bus, and "Blancs" in the rear.

"Sounds like the Pompey train to London on Friday night where submariners had their own compartments. Never worked out why", says Lofty looking skyward.

Tolerating another interruption, Dave continues

"Durban was a wonderful city could be called the 'Surfer's Paradise of South Africa"

"Dave, I thought you said it was a nice place" says Tezza, pushing Dave's patience to the limit.

A frown on Dave's face gives expression to his disapproval of the sarcasm and interruption to his story.

"An amazing town, which had more Holden cars than Sydney, and ninety-five percent of the Durban Fire Brigade, were Australians. They introduced us to the 'Smugglers Inn' bar at the Alexandra Hotel, which was where all the tourists, in particular the rich country girls from Bloemfontein, Johannesburg and Rhodesia, used to drink and party.

"The best hotel in town was 'The Four Seasons' where we stayed. My Rhodesian friend was woken up at 6am by a blood curdling scream from the street."

"Hold the phone; what's this Rhodesian friend thing? says Tezza

"Probably had 4 legs, you how Dave liked wildlife then as per his time in Gibraltar". says Lofty,

"Yeh the blood curdling scream was probably its mother looking for it again." says Tezza.

"Nah, I reckon it was Big Jim the steward in his undies on the balcony. That'd scare the shit out of anyone" says Lofty.

"Are you two finished" says Dave with a look of frustration on his face.

"Anyway, let me continue. We raced to the window and there was a Zulu Warrior in all his feathers and regalia, pulling a passenger cart, jumping up and down and emitting fierce war cries"

"Don't tell me, Big Jim was in the cart in his undies refusing to pay?" said Lofty

Dave's frown showed his frustration as he finished his story,

"Scared the shit out of the two of us so much that we had to go back to bed for the rest of the day" says Dave with a naughty smile on his face

"AHH, nothing like Bovine love affairs." says Tezza

"Piss off Tezza" says Dave throwing a cushion at the pair of gigglers whilst pouring a tot of rum for each of them.

The night went on for some time with the stories bouncing back and forth and the rum and port bottles rapidly emptying. The music from the 60's echoed around the place and a fire pit was put together by the now drunk threesome.

Lofty had attended to a neighbours noise protests and the usual ceremonial submariner activities and singing that usually came about when submariners gathered in one place with the right lubrication. Sometime during the night untold mischief befell the gated community before the three rascals collapsed somewhere in the early hours of the next day.

The collective hangover arose in mid-morning and after a difficult breakfast and several technicolor yawns and a tidy up with Dave, the lads were back on the road leaving Dave to explain to his irate neighbours the finer points of the dance of the flamers and why it was essential to perform it in the backyard late last night.

Meanwhile Tezza had managed to burn his butt by using a cellophane wrapper instead of newspaper as is the norm and was now sitting side saddle as Lofty drove down the suburban street heading for the highway and giggling to himself. He wasn't aware that he still had a feather in his hair plucked from the neighbour's prize chook that became a midnight barbeque item. Bloody Lofty will eat anything thought Tezza.

Dave had hastily packed a few buns and some cold meat left over from the Barbequed prize chook that Lofty had made for dinner. A short while down the road, Tezza was keen to get some treatment for his lightly toasted rear end, the pair decided it was time for an early lunch and perhaps a picnic was in order. A suitable rest stop came into view and the car pulled up near a picnic table.

The place was deserted except for a grey nomad couple sitting proudly under their pull-out awning drinking tea and large truck further down the layby.

THE PICNIC

The chicken didn't look that appealing but the bread rolls were well buttered (as you do when you're half pissed) so the pair took only one each deciding to stick to fluids to quench the hangover.

"Lofty, you know we will have to ring up Dave's missus and apologise" says Tezza.

"For what", says Lofty, looking indignant.

"The dance of the flamers for one. Then there was the mess we made trying to wash our clothes." says Tezza.

"Not my fault; I thought that was washing stuff not doggy bubble bath"

"Well then what about the neighbour's sprinklers that you turned around so they were all aimed at their front door", says Tezza.

"They were not impressed this morning when they were hosed down after you ringing the doorbell."

"Well, it worked didn't it, the whining bastards have no taste in music. Anyway, that's a trick I learnt from Sandy who watched them install automatic sprinklers at Sunnyvale and found a way to interfere with the programming. I just revered the sensor to go on when it detects motion rather than off. Then I put the sprinklers on jet mode and opened the pressure limiting valves wide open" says Lofty feeling very proud of himself.

"Okay, Mr. Urban Terrorist, I don't want the details" say Tezza expecting a long- winded explanation of Lofty's commando raid on Dave's neighbour who now couldnt go out their front door without getting soaked.

"Anyway, who was it that decided to camouflage the car with Dave's prize dahlias. His Missus is gonna go apeshit when she sees those all pulled up". says Lofty,

"I did kind of put them back but, don't you start Lofty. Dave will be picking baked beans off his ceiling for weeks after that explosion you caused this morning" says Tezza

"How was I to know you had to open the cans before you put them on the stove? Anyway, the dog seemed to enjoy the fallout." says Lofty

"Gawd, bloody Coxswains, that's another thing. Why did you give the dog a bloody haircut?" says Lofty smiling from ear to ear,

"Well, it didn't look right; even though Dave said it had been to the doggy parlor and it cost a fortune to have it clipped I reckoned it was a lousy job." says Tezza

"Yeh well now its bloody bald you idiot" says Lofty smiling.

"Alright, so I was a bit enthusiast and pissed at the time, but I had greyhounds for a few years, and I always clipped them close when needed." Says Tezza looking skyward

"Yep, I remember the dog shit in the back of the wagon. So what are we gonna do mate." chides Lofty.

"No problem we'll blame Dave, easy." says Tezza,

"Yeh!! "I get it, we were on duty, right." says Lofty

The pair burst into laughter whilst holding their heavily hung-over heads, burnt arse and chook feather hairdo's. Tezza recovered himself and spoke.

"Mate, I've got to do something about my burnt arse it is killing me.

By my reckoning we are about 2 hours from the next town but I can't wait that long, I will see if we have a first aid kit" says Tezza grimacing and holding his burnt bum and rummaging in the car boot to no avail.

"What the hell is this" says Tezza pointing to a rather large fiberglass fish that's poking its head out from under a pile of rubbish and clothing.

"Oh, that I forgot about that. That's a souvenir Dolphin a pinched whilst you were adjusting the gate sign last night." says Lofty,

Judging by the look of disbelief on Tezza face, Lofty explains.

"Don't you remember, you swapped the letters around on the gate sign and pinched a few from the visitors parking only sign to make the Earls Gate entrance sign read Pearly Gates. Then we pinched this fish and set the other one up with the fountain coming out of its arse."

"Can't have been me, I was on duty and besides that's a Japanese Carp not a dolphin you knocked off" says Tezza

"Really, never mind they're a pest aren't they so we did them a favour eh!" says Lofty

"I can't take you anywhere can I, now back to my sore bum." says Tezza

"Don't worry mate, I've heard that butter is good so let's rub the butter of into those buns in your arse crack. That would at least soothe it and then perhaps put some rags onto it." Says Lofty looking serious

With no alternative Tezza decides the idea was better than none and proceeds to drop his trousers and bends over the picnic table whilst Lofty opens a couple of the well buttered buns.

Tezza had just begun rubbing the buttery bun into his burnt arse crack when a minibus full of women pulls into the rest stop directly opposite the pair near the toilets. The door flies open, and half a dozen women spill out onto the roadway looking for the toilets.

The scene that greeted the ladies of Tezza wiping a bread roll up his arse crack whilst Lofty stood nearby munching on another bun left the ladies aghast. Tezza paused with his bum facing the assembled ladies stopped rubbing a bun up and down his arse crack whilst Lofty (always hungry) standing beside him kept munching on his bun.

"You two! comes a shout from one of the women in the crowd of old chooks. "What the hell do you think you're doing?"

It was Dave's wife returning from her day away on the minibus. Tezza, embarrassed by his exposure, pulled up his pants and headed for the car leaving Lofty to saunter back to the car still munching on the bread roll.

"Sorry ladies, just stopped for a shit sandwich, hope you don't mind, want a bite."

The aghast group of ladies disappear rapidly toward the toilets muttering to themselves, disgusting, perverts, obscene.

Walking behind as the other ladies' scurry toward the haven of the lady's toilet, Daves Missus issues a final comment over her shoulder.

"You guys had better not have been to my house or I'll kill the pair of you and hang that lunatic hubby of mine out to dry. Remember, we are going to see you at the reunion.

Getting back into the driver's seat Lofty says to Tezza.

"Mate I hope Dave has cleaned up and paid off the neighbors before she gets home."

"Yeh, but do you reckon she will notice that the Bali room has burnt down." says Tezza

"Bound to mate, you know how women have an eye for detail and that palm frond thing we stuck together this morning whilst Dave was in bed won't pass muster." says Lofty

"Anyway, we were duty, weren't we" says Tezza,

Laughter continues for some time and the butter seemed to have eased Tezzas burnt bum problems as they headed off toward their destination.

The scenery had changed somewhat since the pair crossed the border and dinnertime found them happily sitting in a booth at an eatery called Boomers. So named supposedly because the waitress's had their back sides exposed and displayed an ample amount of bosom.

The lads enjoyed the food, and the eye candy and discussions naturally flowed to the delights of the female form and the possible uses it could be put to.

"Mate, you know at our age ambition far exceeds our capability" says lofty

"That's true and I agree mate but it's still good to go window shopping from time to time." says Tezza

"So long as the missus doesn't catch you" says Lofty.

They both agreed that times had changed and that even their discussions had all the signs of falling into the dirty old man category. Lofty continues,

"Your quite right Tezza, I've noted my conversations with others had changed over time. I used to discuss football, beer and sex (not always in that order). These days it's more likely to be Doctors, pills and the sale of sensible shoes that occupy me. I must admit trying to change the style of conversation with a bunch of old blokes I met at a bowling club. After hearing all the usual pill discussions, shoes etc. etc. I decided it was time to strike."

"Can't wait to hear this one" says Tezza.

"Lofty explains his interaction at a bowling club.

"I bet she's good with balls," I said loudly, pointing at a lady bowler bending over to deliver her bowling ball down the green. There was a silence around the table so I jumped back in "I bet I could upset her aim Phew" pointing at a not too bad looking 50 something walking towards the bowling green.

"You really let em have it didn't you Lofty" says Tezza laughing loudly at the scene in his head.

"Yes, but it all backfired mate" says Lofty.

"It appeared that the 2 ladies of my desire were related in some way to the gathering of men folk. I don't think I'll go back there for a while. They still point at me in the shops and whisper." says Lofty looking a little sad

"Anyway, what the hell were you doing at a bowling club" says Tezza

"I heard they had free beer for bowlers on Wednesday, so I thought I can chuck a couple of balls around for free beer" says Lofty grinning

"No doubt about you mate. I remember rescuing you from those Jock birds who thought you were looking up their kilts" says, Tezza.

"Well, I was, that was the best sport the Scots ever invented mate" says Lofty.

It was soon time to find somewhere for the night and to grab a bite to eat. As usual Dinner dragged on longer than expected and it was past midnight before the lads were back in their room and peacefully snoring after a hectic day and the effects of mild hangover. Tezza's backside had eased a bit with the application of some ointment they picked up in town trying to explain the problem to a bemused chemist lady.

There was no mischief planned or otherwise as the two old guys were getting more tired as the trip went on. They had agreed to limit their hours on the road to take more time to rest. Waking up late the next day, they enjoyed a modest breakfast that did not suit Lofty but he figured it was for the best if it meant he would forego the mid-morning sleep and miss the scenery which was improving with every kilometre travelled.

POLITICAL CORRECTNESS

On the road again with Tezza at the helm the road slipped away as they chatted about football, beer and women in that order. The day passed uneventfully and Tezza's backside had apparently settled down with the ointment treatment.

The time passed quickly with the usual stops and a lunch break. It was soon time again to find a place for the night. The boys knew they would be in trouble now as the wives had expected their little road trip to only last 2 days and here, they were still on the road on day 4. But they were having fun and there was no way they were going to hurry. Besides, they had a few days before the Vets convention.

The sun had long departed when they pulled into run down looking motel on the edge of a small town off the main road. The motel looked like something out of horror movie and the room was just as threatening but it was right next door to a services club so they figured it would be a good place to have dinner and a few beers.

Being mid-week the club was almost empty except the diehard pokie fans and the distant sounds of a one-man band plonking away in the club lounge. After an unexciting parmajarma and chips the lads headed back to the fleabag motel and early night. The adventures of the past few days had taken their toll on the boys were not as resilient as they once were.

After showering and reclining on their beds the pair soon realised that sleep would not come easy. Tezza and Lofty were both unusually quiet and both appeared to be contemplating something. They always seemed to be on the same wavelength and it is possible they were thinking about the same thing.

POLITICAL CORRECTNESS FOR OLD FARTS

After some banter the lads get down to another meaty subject.

"you know, you can't call a young lady who served us a coffee this morning Luv anymore due to this WOKE crap. says Tezza

Im confused and worried about this politically correct WOKE stuff. Lofty I know how much you subscribe to WOKENESS and political correctness so maybe you can explain it to me, says Tezza with a smile on his face.

"Me!, politically correct! Yeh right, thought we sorted that out years ago, the only thing I would caution against in this age of political correctness is we old blokes need to be mindful of the sensitivities of the young ones and the not so young generations". says Lofty with a sneer,

"Its out of hand, says Lofty, for instance. don't try comforting a crying child or you will be up on molestation charges before you can blink. Even bouncing a grandchild on your knee can bring looks of disdain from the politically correct faction of society despite explanations." says Lofty

"You seem to understand the rules better than me, says Tezza. But apart from that, we must face that past 60 years of age we enter the age of invisibility and become patronised beyond reality. We are easier to manipulate as we are seen as harmless. That also requires us to make more regular visits to the medical profession for one reason or another." says Tezza

Lofty, nodding his agreement vigorously.

"However, Im confused about this gender and pronoun thing they all go on about." Says Tezza

"Easy, just call yourself what you want and be what you want. Im using the pronoun of Fido and want to live like a dog. Sit on the lounge all day, lick my balls, fart so bad that it clears the room. Bang on the door and bark in the middle of the night to go out then shit on the neighbours lawn and piss on his leg when he protests." says Lofty

"So what's different? Isn't that what you do now anyway?? Says Tezza

"Smart arse. Okay so whats your pronoun thingy" says Lofty

"Me, Im going to be called Tiddles, and live like a cat. None of that ball chasing stuff you've got to do, I will sit around and control the house, go out catting all night and sleep all day. Just the odd fur ball, but unlike you who must go outside I have the indoor cat litter dunny " says Tezza smirking and preening like a cat

"That sounds like you mate. How's the wife like using the kitty litter thing" say Lofty holding his nose

They both burst into laughter and carry on with the nonsense.

"You know the way the Woke Brigade has found a need to make old terms politically incorrect? So, let's discuss how some of the terms have been changed over the years. I'll kick them off," says Tezza

"Can you recall when accountants became financial controllers? and when doctors and nurses became medical professionals, teachers became knowledge advocates. It's interesting that engineers stayed as engineers but there are more categories now." Says Tezza

"You're right about that, in my day you could become either and electrical, mechanical or civil engineers. Now, who knows. I think it's our fault Tezza that we just let all this stuff go through to the keeper without any pushback. They just keep pushing their BS and we take it and roll over. Some of the nuanced titles really get me going." says Lofty

"I agree with that. "Baldness is now hair follicle depletion," says Tezza, scratching his thinning hair. Lofty deep in thought comes back with,

"Deafness, is hearing impaired or audibility receipt challenged" says Lofty

"That's a bit deep mate" says Tezza.

A period of silence ensues whilst the pair is deep in thought and the miles fly past. The silence is broken when Tezza says,

"How about false teeth as dental enhancement and oral refurbished implements"

"Good one Tezza were on a roll now. What about glasses as vision rectification devices."

Laughter ensues as Lofty pretends to peer over the steering wheel.

"Beer belly is now physiological and gravitational effects", says Tezza quickly.

More laughter, pointing at Lofties paunch.

"More like a keg with a tap than a six pack now mate" says Tezza.

Lofty points at Tezzas nether regions.

"Okay, cop this one

"Erections problems now sexually restrained and blood restricted vital organ", that's us, says lofty pointing to his nether regions also

"That's a bit unkind mate, have you been talking to my missus" says Tezza.

"No mate, Mine."

Laughter erupts as Tezza says,

"Yeh I've been talking to your missus too. Pissing your pants she calls impromptu bladder release."

Got you there mate says Tezza with a smile on his face.

"Yes but the last time I spoke to your missus she mentioned your Limp dick problems. Upwardly challenged reproductive device." says, Lofty

"Alright, alright, I think we have explored our inner secrets enough. says Tezza

Lofty pipes in with his crowning piece to the discussion

"To put that into a typical scenario of an old bloke like me who is balding, deaf on one side, wears glasses and has a beer belly (the rest I'm not admitting to). I'm quite happy to fess up to being a Bald, deaf, half blind fat old bastard. In fact, I'm almost proud of that title, at least it means I've worn out a few body parts.

"However, I'm not happy with the politically correct version of my worn-out old body which would be, hair follicle depleted, audibly challenged and physiological and gravitational effected with vision rectification devices. What a mouthful of BS that is." says Lofty

"I couldn't live with that mouthful either, no wonder with our growing list of deficiencies we become targets for this type of stuff." says Tezza,

"To escape this sort of crap some of us become extroverts. yes, we know you look cool in your sports car with your fake ponytail blowing in the wind, false orange, tan, gold chain and rent a bride, but really is it necessary or did you just miss out on this stuff when you were young? says Tezza,. Feigning a gesture of admiration for himself.

"That's, definitely not me, but there are some good ideas there" says Lofty.

Tezza holding up his hand

"Alright, that's good for you but others like me become introverts and virtual hermits. Bah Humbug becoming the normal exchange with relatives and friends. A kind of remorse sets in and then a pattern that cannot be broken. Bingo Thursday, meat raffle Friday etc. The introverted old fart must follow the routine regardless." explains Tezza

"Tezza, did you take your vitamins this morning mate. Thats not you? says Lofty,!

"I know, I know I was just giving you an opposite position OK," says Tezza hands held in the air.

"Wouldn't it be good if we could find a middle ground between making fools of ourselves and turning into grumpy old men"? Says Lofty.

"I have tried but with varying levels of success but some of the problems of being an old bloke come back to haunt me. I've set out to find some middle ground or equilibrium in my lifestyle". say Tezza.

"Just don't ask me to dance with you OK" says Lofty

GENE THEORY

Reflecting on their travels through the beautiful coastal hinterlands, Lofty expresses his opinion on the relationship between genes and conscience. noticing the look on Tezzas face which says here we go again. Lofty decides to push on.

"Let me explain, who gave us this bloody encumbrance called a conscience that has things like a work ethic and duty built in, I never asked for it, did you?" says Lofty looking quizzical.

"I sense Im going to find out whether I want to or not" says Tezza putting his head in his hands briefly

"Ok Chief, It's a long story but since you aren't going anywhere strap yourself in and I will explain." says Lofty with a fatherly glace at his mate

"When we are born there must be various genes we are given. My missus got in the wrong que. As they handed out the drinking gene they said this line was for those on the brink of success, but she thought they said she was to drink to excess and thus they scrubbed her when she turned up pissed". says Lofty

A slight giggle arose as Tezza tips in

"I know what you mean. Certain genes must be natural for care givers, priests and Nuns and people with those sorts of futures like my Missus who failed the entrance exam but still practices as a nun. she confused celebrate with celibate and did just that in other words, I get none." Says Tezza

A smile crosses both their faces.

Lofty goes on.

"There are those who get the arsehole gene, like traffic cops, they must go to a special school for arseholes as they grow up. I think I met a couple of them at my school. They were bullies and big mouthed dickheads.

"Then there are the genes for footballers and heavy contact sporting types but they are well down the pecking order and seem a bit brain damaged from birth. For you and me, and our former navy colleagues we must have the donkey gene as we always seem to be pulling our weight uphill.

"Now of course for every equal there is an opposite and this is where the nasty gene comes in. These genes seem predominant in terrorists, lawyers, politicians, real estate and car salesperson types. But the twist is its not in all of them." said Lofty

"Okay, so where does the conscience come in?" asks Tezza

"Sure, some of us get to add handicaps to genes such as a conscience, not everyone will have one. However, you and I lucked out we got one so we were destined to work for a dollar our entire lives, whereas the oxygen thieves without a conscience don't." says Lofty.

"Spot on" says Tezza.

Continuing his recital

"You must understand that you don't have to suffer from your genes throughout your entire life. If you really pull your weight on request, you can go and work for a wife who will love you for your work ethic. In fact, it's probably in the husband hunting checklist, work ethic high etc." says Lofty lowering his sunglasses on his nose whilst glancing at Tezza like an irritable professor.

A puzzled look crosses Tezza's face,

"Now I'm lost so, please explain" says Tezza sounding like a well known politician

"Okay let me try and clear it up for you. We went to work mainly for the benefits it gave us and the money we could earn, right" says Lofty

Tezza nods agreement so Lofty charges on

"Ok but does that motive mean I'm bad or maybe a little arsehole gene has crept in?" says Lofty

"No problem" says Tezza,

"Unfortunately, the mess can't be undone, so outside of shooting you, and to save face with the genes provider many react and lose their inhibitions or suspend them. With this flexibility in their genes they often rise to higher ranks in the military, and the bigger dick head that he or she is the higher up the corporate ladder they will go. So, when you go to bed tonight ask yourself what genes did, I get?" says Tezza

Now they are both laughing uncontrollably, so much so that Lofty must pull over to the side of the road.

"No doubt about us, we are still great bullshitters mate" says Tezza.

After a light lunch the duo decided to deviate from the main highway and look at the countryside. The car pulled slowly onto a dusty road shared with huge trucks and the dust t made the first few km's difficult. Tezza couldn't escape the driving duties for the next leg of the road trip but regretted it as soon as he pulled out between behemoth sized trucks full of dusty stuff.

The subject turned to finances and how they had arrived at successful retirement positions.

"Hope you're going to wash the car at the next stop" says, Lofty.

A wry look from the over-stressed Tezza gave him the answer he thought he would get. It was late in the afternoon when they decided it was time to stop and rest for the night. Neither was keen on night driving and besides they were having a good time. The turn off to a small town looked like the opportunity to find a motel and something to eat as well as a long hot shower.

SWINGERS

The country inn looked good and it had a restaurant as well so they booked and after a long shower and a clothing sort out they headed for the restaurant and enjoyed steak and some wine. The restaurant was quiet except for several couples who kept staring at the lads for some reason.

A waiter answered Tezza's question as he explained it's a queers and queens swingers gathering and they're all wondering if you're going to join them later. Lofty nearly choked on his pudding and Tezza looked past the waiter to the smiling couples.

Grabbing Lofty he says,

"Come on mate, we are out of here" as he leads the still choking Lofty back to the room and locks the door.

"What was all that about swingers' mate" says Lofty

"Don't ask, I think we were going to be part of the fresh meat or entertainment for that bunch of weirdos". Says Tezza

"I don't know, mate, a couple of those sheilas looked ok to me" says Lofty

"I'm sure they did to you but they were all males. It was a queens and queers swap meet weekend according to the waiter. says Tezza

"OOOOH! I see leave me out then" says Lofty.

Without further discussion the two old vets got into bed only to be woken later in the evening by the sounds of moaning and crying from the rooms on either side. A restless night and lack of sleep saw them on the road early. A quick breakfast at a roadside diner some distance from town and they were back on the road and mulling over the swinger's thing and how that might work in practice.

RETIREMENT CONSPIRACY

The road rolled on and discussions turned to more mundane things with Lofty breaking the silence

" Youve done pretty well for yourself mate. What about sharing your wisdom on retirement finances with me Tezza" says, Lofty.

"Lofty my take on retiring is a bit jaundiced. I've had a lot of time to think about it but as you've been travelling from one side of the continent to the other in your working life, I suppose you had a different take to mine which was mandated by the Navy pension fund. Weve both somehow managed to retire successfully I think and I'm supposing your road to that success would be more exciting than mine" says Tezza

"Sure, happy to share what I can remember but I've come up with a Theory that might explain it better" says Lofty.

"I'm all ears" said Tezza with a wry grin on his face and concentration focused on the dirt road ahead.

Lofty begins his explanation

"Paul Kelly wrote a song that had lyrics that went something like: 'Have you ever seen Sydney from a 747 at night.' Well, picture this, it's a Friday night and I'm on this 737 and the view is similar in row 27 to any other row. Here I am amongst the dark-suited army of worn-out business refugees descending into a dazzle of lights and the promises a city at night offers the traveler.

"That's a bit deeper than I thought, so what's it got to do with retiring," says Tezza

"Hang in there chief and I will explain the analogy; there's a similarity between approaching to land in an aircraft to pre-retirement planning. Like the city emerging below us, on the face of it retiring looks great. Bright lights, enjoyment, and plans of relaxing more are the focus. Just like the brochures for that god awful place we live in. Happy fit older people doing interesting things. Am I ready for this stuff, you bet!"

Lofty continues

"That's fine I think to myself. I'll never look like those guys in the brochure, wouldn't mind the missus looking like some of those women though. But then the fear sets in as we make our final approach to the runway known as pre-retirement planning, then into the terminal grab your bags and .... Now what

"I think I'm following you says Tezza"

"If like me mate you hadn't thought this far ahead and who hasn't regretted some moves weve made pre-retirement at our age, you probably availed yourself of a Yoda-like guru known as a retirement advisors. Now these are basically good folk, well-intentioned and in the main very knowledgeable. I just wish they had started shaving or at least that their voices had changed before they gave out advice.

The message I get is clear.

You don't have enough money to retire until you are 90 my Yoda told me.

"But hang on Yoda I tell him...I did as the force told me, put money into superannuation, bought a reasonable house, had a reasonably well-paid job. So, what went wrong? Now Star Wars has begun. Out comes the computer screen and smiling freshly unbraced toothy smile from my Yoda, as he gave me 20 minutes of what went wrong. Seems I should have been having this chat when I left school

Tezza chimes in breaking Lofty's train of thought.

"It's easy mate, sell some assets and go live in a shack in the mountains and live off roadkill and weeds or something." He says

Shaking his head, Lofty explains.

"Mate, he tells me that's not an option; the Government won't allow that either. Is there anything I can do I ask??

"Die young maybe" said, Tezza?

A look of disdain crosses Loftys face as they continue down the dusty road at a good pace.

"Ok, Lofty so what were the options. Retire at 90, tell lies to the government or rob a bank. The latter is out because there aren't many of them around anymore and you need a gun to get served anyway". said, Tezza

"Too true ole son says Lofty but lets' get back to the smiling Yoda"

Interrupting again Tezza chimes in with

"There is an option, use the force Lofty"

"No doubt about it, you're on fire today, but no, my Yoda had a solution." said Lofty with a broad smile on his face

"Remembering I was 59 at the time, all I needed to do was to put away about $55,000 + a year for the next 10 years to catch up. Great., that'll work, I said to my Yoda. I will just go home tell the wife she will have to cut back on takeaway roadkill because I'm going to put 90% of my wages into the super fund. I should just about have enough left to get to and from work. This means I work 6 months of the year for the Government and the other 6 months for my super fund. Wow, now I'm excited.

"So back to bank robbery maybe" said, Tezza

"After another 30 minutes of 'consultation' where charts flash on and off screens quicker than an X fighter and the dialogue sounds more like R2D2 speak than English, I staggered out of Yoda's cave with an arm full of brochures and charts and things that are supposed to be my pre-retirement financial plan. I'm sure I heard Yoda's mother calling him home for dinner as I left." said Lofty

"Well, at least you got something to take home to show the missus you weren't in the pub all afternoon." Says Tezza

"Now don't get me wrong says Lofty, these Yoda's types are clever and they are necessary. Some are even helpful if you know the language. At this stage I was a middle-aged ignoramus when it came to finances. Sure, I can drive a aircraft and have sailed the seven seas and done the odd bit of management but I can't get my head around the whole retirement thing at this stage. I don't think I'm alone judging by the stupefied look on others faces leaving Yoda's cave." says Lofty

Tezza adds his thoughts.

"Perhaps someone out there has the answer to the promised retirement we all thought we were owed when we set out on this journey in the 50s and 60's. Where did it all go wrong or is it just us poor idiots who kept their nose to the grindstone and failed to keep up." Says Tezza

"All that shit was going through my head on the plane." Says Lofty

"The announcement brings me back to reality with a jolt in row 27, putting my seat in the upright position and stowing my tray table. Looking around at my fellow travelers I realize I am sitting in the pre-retirement rows at the back of the plane. Is this some sort of conspiracy? Put all the old tired buggers down the back, they delay the upwardly mobiles disembarking. No, it is just a Friday night flight full of worn out 50 something's desperately hanging on till redundancy, heart attack or Yoda comes along to save them." Says Lofty

"Geez, mate you've got me depressed now. Please tell me you worked it out because here we are now retired" said, Lofty

"Do I have any answers? not really, am I bitter? probably. Will I survive? Definitely. Perhaps we have come to expect too much out of retirement or perhaps it has all got too complicated to the point where we shut down. Perhaps it's just a fact that so many of us are trying to find a safe harbor to park our Xwing fighters. I think I will be alright so long as I'm dead before I turn 78. May the force be with you, says Lofty popping another mint in his mouth.

THE AGE OF INVISIBILITY

Whilst we are about retirement and technology and before I piss my pants again laughing let me tell you what we've been up to in the technological stakes at our place.

"The missus decided we would upgrade our stuff when we retired" says Tezza.

"Don't tell me you've still got that steam-powered TV you miserable old prick" says Lofty.

"Mate you know I never throw stuff out but our old miniature TV and other stuff was getting on and it couldn't be fixed when it broke so it was time for some new junk" replied Lofty.

"Thanks to our son we have a 52" LCD TV which talks to our telephone. The telephone is a THub (whatever that is) and is connected to our internet and this is connected to our Movie stream computer that downloads TV programs we like and alerts us to upcoming movies we might want to watch.

"The THub is a flat screen thing that works like an IPad and with much the same functionality and is wireless. I'm told it will even talk to my refrigerator. But hey, there's nothing in there that will answer back I hope, so what's the point of that?"

Both laugh thinking about their own fridges and days gone past at some of the diabolical food that came out of them.

Lofty continues,

"Daily I work from home on a CAD (computer aided design) system that interacts globally with another specialist when we work on designs and concepts. I've never met these folks but I figure if they are as possessed by the computer demon as I am then maybe I wouldn't want to meet them."

"You're in fantasy land again Lofty," says Tezza

"You think that's fantasy land, I recently had the pleasure of seeing a military combat system in action which has a lot of the drop and drag features we see on futuristic videos. Even though I didn't have a clue what was going on (the military love jargon and acronyms) it blew me away with its accuracy and complexity. I guess they were not amused when I asked where the batteries went and how many 10-year-olds they were recruiting who could operate this stuff." says Lofty

Both laugh again

"I guess what I'm saying is the stuff of dreams we see on videos is not that far off. Do we need it?? do we want it??? Is it progress???" Says Tezza

Oh God here comes another bloody sermon thinks Lofty holding his head in his hands.

"Mate, I often need help to find a TV station on the remote control. Then with 121 stations to choose from it all gets too hard and I go pick up a book. The other day when my 5-year-old granddaughter started showing me her games on an IPhone I thought it's time to quit and admit I'm getting run over by the technology I need to use to survive. I'm sure our kids and others will take all this in their stride and hopefully, we will not need to bother." Says Tezza frowning

"Tezza, your right, and I'm the same. Something to ask your brood of females mate. Ask them if they buy their clothes off a computer screen without the aid of a shop assistant, given the level of service is the same everywhere i.e. none. Maybe it's that we become invisible once we turn a certain age. Hello, hello, is anybody out there" says Lofty??

"Mate, I think we are both too old for the new age and we should just let it all go past us" says Tezza.

The exchange over with no resolution, the pair retire to their respective corners of the car and enjoy the vista of sea and sun that the north coast has to offer. Finally, the silence is too much for the pair of old windbags and Tezza breaks the silence with a well-planned fart and exclamation.

"That one hurt" says Tezza

"I don't bloody wonder. Best we stop so you can unload whatever it is that has died up there" says Lofty winding down his window.

After a quick trip to the loo and stretching their legs the lads get back on the road and proceed north again.

"What time is lunch" enquires Lofty,

"The same as yesterday, about 2 hours after we stop for morning tea and you fill your face with stodge. says Tezza

"No stodge today. Today we eat wholesome, no sticky buns and a healthy lunch in the Couth Resi, says Lofty.

"You won't last Lofty so stop dreaming," says Tezza with a smirk on his face

"I betcha I will and to support that If I don't, I'll shout lunch"

"Cheeky bugger, it's your turn anyway" says Tezza slapping Lofty on the arm. Tezza very quickly realised he can't win but agrees wholeheartedly.

The scenery remains beautiful and the boys sit back and enjoy the ride. Down the track Lofty comments,

"Tezza I have an opinion about our conversations on this trip but I want yours,"

"Fire away Lofty", Says Tezza feeling just a little curious and half expecting another raft of Loftys philosophical downloads

"Well, since we set out on this road trip we have talked about a lot of stuff, right"

"Agreed" says Tezza,

"So, my question is what's been the main topics of our discussions, almost to the exclusion of all others have we covered." Says Lofty looking a little worried at having asked the question

"I'm curious as to why you're asking but it's a no brainer. Well, not in any order, my take on it, would be sex, food, booze and friendship" says Tezza

"Bugger me mate you have nailed my thoughts exactly" says Lofty.

"I can't think of any reason why they are not the chart toppers. Now, if the ladies were here it would be different, the subjects that we have discussed so far would put us in a dangerous position, so instead we would have to concentrate on the road and do our best to ignore them, true" says, Tezza.

Not sure about danger, how so" says Lofty,

"Well, like in danger of nodding off and wiping ourselves out," says Tezza

"Yep I can see that certainly comes under the realm of danger says Lofty,

Tezza now in full flight extends the concept of danger with a flourish of his hands.

"Just imagine what we avoided by not having them along on this road trip. The danger of finally having to comment on their shitty nappy days or days of our lives talk or even their slant on politics, heaven help us, to the point we cannot stand it any longer and call them morons and that would put us in line for neutering and finish our sex lives for our remaining time in this world but also in the next as well most likely.

That's assuming that the bloke upstairs has delved into his bag of humour tricks and set the policy that marriage is for eternity and not just as a seemingly horrible and ghastly earthly experience and boy if that not's dangerous what is, imagine not being able to max yourself to end it all" says Tezza getting worked up

"Mate, I didn't know you felt that way about your marriage but married throughout eternity, please, let's not go there" says Lofty.

"Got ya, Im getting as big a bullshitter as you and I've just passed the Lofty test of believability says Tezza.

"So that meandering monologue on marriage and your marriage was all BS? asks Lofty

"Right, lucky I recorded it then" says Lofty pointing to his phone

A scramble for Lofty's phone nearly sends the car off the road. As the pair settle down and a smile comes across Lofty's face.

"Never try to bullshit a master bullshitter chief. Got you going though didn't I" says Lofty

"I swear one day Im going to beat you at that game. Anyway, hows your hunger going" says Tezza smiling back at his friend.

Lofty tightened his belt as the pair bypassed roadhouse signs and food stalls although it was noted that he was into the chocolates in the glove box that Tezza forgot to get rid of. Tezza was happy to bypass as many food outlets as possible and the pair went silent with Lofty sulking and complaining of lack of nutrients to fuel his large frame.

It wasn't long before the turn off to the town of Couth came into sight and the expectation of fine lunch.

RESTAURANT MAYHEM

The restaurant was a very formal one and was not the place to go for a cheap nosh. Still, it was lunch and Lofty was paying so they went in.

Tezza decided that a visit to the restroom was in order and left Lofty to order something for lunch.

"What would you like," Lofty asked.

"Oh, you know me, anything healthy and filling as I'm starving" was his reply.

That presented a problem as Lofty couldn't read the menu as he didn't speak Swahili, as it appeared to be written in. It was also clear the place was no longer a steak house, but there were quite nice little symbols alongside things.

Lofty was hoping for some help from the waitress who promptly appeared as the place was almost empty. Never a good sign.

Lofty was starving as it had been some hours since the pair enjoyed a light breakfast . Tezza was nowhere to be seen and the waitress was becoming anxious to get the order. Okay, this is it, just dive in and ask the silly questions and hope you understand the answers thinks Lofty.

"What is this here' he asked pointing to the menu. The answer came back in what sounded like Swahili. It turns out that the restaurant was staffed by itinerant backpackers who spoke neither Swahili nor English but what sounded like a mixture of both to Lofty. After some sign language, Lofty manages to get Manuela (they never found out her real name) to get the manager over.

"Gad moaning slur, cu nee hull you" was the greeting Lofty heard from behind him.

It was the manager who must be a Cuban refugee with an expressed the desire to go to America someday and pursue his singing career. Lofties first mistake was to ask him about that notion, to which he replied, "ohm me goodness slur, I sung floor you" to which Lofty was treated to 3 choruses of when the saints come marching in. The other waiters then insisted in joining in thinking this was what was wanted and as there weren't any other customers so why not.

Tezza returns and berates Lofty for not having ordered despite having attracted a barber shop quartet around the table. And disappears again to look for someone who could speak English in the hope that he will rescue the situation and they will finally get some food.

The Waiters cacophony finished with a flourishing of trays and everyone departing without so much as bread sticks being left behind. Waiters seemed to be swooping majestically in and out of the kitchen but nothing seemed to be happening. After almost tackling one of these elusive swooping waiters Lofty managed to get some attention.

A young waitress with plats and buck teeth was cornered at the table by Lofty.

"I want to order some food please; can you take my order" he said in a rather loud voice.

"The young thing looked at him and burst into tears disappearing into the kitchen.

Great thought Lofty, no food but I've managed to upset a waitress which is always bad unless you don't mind having your food compromised by the introduction of foreign objects and the like.

Then out of the kitchen comes the biggest meanest looking hulk of a man in a dirty chef's uniform, heading Lofties way.

"so" he says in a menacing way with a broad foreign accent, standing over Lofty like a nasty volcano about to explode

"yoo wan to fook my girl" he says with a vengeance.

"What," says Lofty looking very sheepish and apologetic?

"No, no I want to order food" gesturing toward his mouth. Godzilla raises himself up even higher and says.

"You do not talk dirty sex talk to my gal, get out"

Eventually, Tezza returns to find Lofty outside looking through the window at him. Many hand signals later and Tezza comes outside and asks what he is doing skulking outside.

Lofty explains and Tezza really goes off the planet. "What were you thinking asking that young girl for sex, have you no shame, she is barely 18 you dirty old scoundrel. It was the plats wasn't it"

Despite Lofties protestations and explanations it appears Tezza is not going to listen. Lofty peered through the window as Tezza appeared to explain the situation to the manager from Cuba and his singing partners and everyone then got up and marched outside.

Tezza begins by asking Lofty what he had said to the girl and where it all went wrong whilst the barbershop quartet glared angrily at Lofty. It seems that the whole misunderstanding revolved around the word food. Anyway, it was apparent the pair was not going to eat there today even if they would serve them, so it was into the car and off down the road to a small café that Lofty remembers as having reasonable food.

Now this looked like Lofty's kind of place too. There was a long counter and little booths to sit in. The menu was on a big blackboard and even though the language seemed like the one down the road, Tezza assured lofty that this place was good.

There seemed to be a lot of activity in the place which is always a good sign for a hungry traveler. However, the diners all looked a bit weird to Lofty, but hey he'd eaten with submariners and you don't get any weirder than that.

Thank God Tezza stepped up to the plate and offered to order for them.

'What will you have," he said.

After an hour wasted at the last place, Lofty was happy to take a back seat. Besides, he still couldn't read the menu. Tezza looks at him and says

"Leave it to me I'll get us something to eat, just sit down and shut up" and then goes to the counter.

Lofty was ready for a burger and chips and Tezza knew that it was his favourite trash food after the McStodge incident earlier on the trip. So Lofty figured Tezza would make him proud with a mountain of cholesterol-enriched stodge.

Lofty wasn't disappointed when the waitress came back with a plate piled up with stodge, just what he wanted. No time for talking with the hunger he had developed. Tezza arrived back at the table with more meager salad looking things in front of him. Lofty figured that's his choice, I'm into this plate of stodge.

After a few bites, Lofty was beginning to wonder what he was eating. The chips were a funny shape and colour and the burger meat was unusual, to say the least. Who cares, Lofty thought, I'm hungry and this is going down ok.

The pair is distracted from their dining by a siren and a blue light which appears to be coming towards the café at some speed. The doors burst open and it's clear from the tone of the law enforcement officer that they are all to stay put.

One of the officers goes to the counter and the other one begins to interrogate the strange looking diners at each table. Tezza explains its some sort of raid as 2 official looking men with plastic bags enter and pair off with the 2 officers.

There is great excitement behind the counter in the kitchen as one of the official looking men with the police holds something up and gestures to the other one. The police officer now gets to Lofty and Tezza's table and asks for ID. The officer explains they are looking for illegal meat substances and the like.

Before they know it Lofty's burger has been seized and bagged by the official who has come back from the kitchen. "Hey that's my lunch arsehole" Lofty exclaims. He had just been getting into that burger and funny-looking chips.

Lofty is arrested with Tezza following him in hot pursuit.

"You just can't keep your mouth shut can you" Can't you see these arseholes don't have a sense of humour?" Says Tezza

That was enough to get Tezza arrested as well. It was 24 hours before the pair could get out of the little cell they were dropped in after Tezza explained to a magistrate what had happened and their innocence in the matter.

The magistrate explained that the police were looking out for two men who were traveling around the district selling illegal meat and they thought we fitted the description.

After their release the pair get back on the road with Lofty curious about the illegal meat issue.

"So, what was the illegal meat thing all about?" said Lofty

"Well, it appears after the recent bushfires some unscrupulous guys got hold of Koala Bear, goanna and snake meat from somewhere then after mixing it they adulterated it with goat urine to preserve the colour and texture, then synthetic flavoring added and it was sold as a form of beef in frozen form.

"So, what the fuck was I eating"? says Lofty

Tezza looking a bit sheepish says.

"Oh, just a regular Koala burger with parnacle chips".

"What the hell are parnacle chips" Lofty ask?

Looking even more sheepish, Tezza replies.

"Oh, they are quite normal softened, deep fired kangaroo claws. You see it's hard to get potatoes here now".

The expletives continue until Lofty has vented his spleen and vowed to stick to McStodges from now on as he gunned the car away from the remote little town.

With a considered expression on his face Tezza recalls the experience

"Lofty that whole experience was like turning back the clock 50 years or so wasn't it; you've got to laugh, don't you?"

"Bullshit how can I laugh I haven't eaten for so long I could eat a shit sandwich," says Lofty

"Yeah right" says Tezza,

"I reckon it would have to have hundreds and thousands on it first."

As the journey continues and the bad food episode is put to bed Tezza decides to change the subject and lighten the atmosphere.

"Anyway, mate stop being so grumpy, you and I have had experiences with towns and their constabulary all over the world, and, as I recall it was usually your fault, we had to present ourselves in front of the beak." says Tezza continuing his thoughts.

"For example, remember Plymouth in the UK, who was it that asked a Bobby (policeman), do you have a pointed head under that pointed hat. Next stop, lock up, and for our pennants remember the brekky, uneatable, it was delivered in a vehicle who some wags painted on it, muck on a truck, apparently it was prepared at the local prison and should have stayed there. Says Tezza"

"If that was supposed to cheer me up you failed, I am still hungry and depressed." says Lofty

"One thing leads to another slim doesn't it" says Tezza.

A LITTLE HUMOUR GOES A LONG WAY

Not giving up on his efforts to cheer Lofty up, Tezza decides on trying some humour.

"Okay, be prepared for humour, stand-by to fill your nappy" says Tezza

"Is that the start of humour. If so back to humour school for you." Says Lofty with a grumble in his voice.

"Settle down grumpy," says Tezza passing Lofty a chocolate bar.

"Here, get your false teeth into this I have been saving it for my grandkids, but you look like you need a chocolate hit to improve your demeanor." Says Tezza

Smirking at Tezza Lofty takes the chocolate and responds.

"Another attempt at humour I suppose, give up. Says Lofty

With a triumphant expression on his face Tezza continues.

"Never, I am on a roll. This will cheer you up or I truly will give up. Here goes, why do brides smile when they are walking down the aisle,

"don't know says Lofty,

"Because they know they have given their last head job," says Tezza

"OK not bad Tezza 7.5, points for that one" says Lofty

"Told you I am on a roll. Try this one. A little kid asks his father, Dad, why do brides wear white, Dad smiles, because all kitchen appliances come in white son," says Tezza

"As per the last one Tezza another 7.5." says Lofty

Continuing his thoughts on the awful jokes Lofty asks Tezza.

"Tezza are you one of those so-called misogynist blokes those jokes are a bit off"

"No, not me, I am very good to my woman, for example when my other half was pregnant, I used to start the lawn mower for her once she was 8 months pregnant."

A small giggle shows he is over his bad mood

"Ok, I am over my grump, no more humour please. What about food topics Tezza or is that off the menu," says Lofty

After some interlude and silence Lofty is feeling better after devouring another chocolate bar Lofty took the initiative,

"My turn Tezza, the subject is now woman and wives" he says.

"Let's go" says Tezza.

WOMEN AND WIVES

With a thoughtful look across at Tezza, Lofty leads the discussion.

"It's not long till we reach the end of this trip, it will be back to the real world and of course reality itself."

"Yep, so what's your point?" says Tezza

"Well, the wives who we know as 'they who must be obeyed' will be there and it's there that we commence our penance for the time we had together. They have had a week to spin stories and excuses over many subjects some of which won't be truthful." Says Lofty

"So, what are you saying, is there something unpleasant in store for us when we get back to our wives Lofty" asks Tezza,

"No just more of the stuff we always get, like 'you're not going out with me looking like that, get changed', or, 'you don't have to get drunk to enjoy yourself,' if they only knew the falsity behind that statement," says Lofty

"Yeah, twin sisters' mate" says Tezza.

"Weve travelled some distance since leaving home both in miles and varied topics, but you know its been great to cover the miles with smiles and remembering our dubious pasts. One day we should write all this down as the grandkids will never believe it and the wives are not likely to tell them as it was." says Tezza

"Good thoughts mate, but my stomach thinks my throats been cut so we have to stopped for something to eat." Says Lofty

They pull into a Grab a Snack Cafe, more commonly known as the GAS Cafe which summed up the effects of a hearty lunch from that place. Still, this was one known to both of the lads and because they served long sandwiches where you picked your own filling, it was a good compromise despite Lofty building a sandwich that needed a ladder to get to the top of.

Still munching on his sandwich, Lofty notices Tezza looking at a map.

"So where to from here" says Lofty

"I was thinking we might head over to the coast again and spend the late afternoon being tourist or something. Besides we need to wash some of our clothes judging by the smell in the car unless you've hidden some roadkill to snack on" says Tezza

"Very funny but I agree lets go over to the coast?" Says Lofty, casually picking the remains of his sandwich out of his teeth.

The next couple of hours they spend winding their way through lush forests and trails arriving at the beachside tourist town.

THE FASHIONISTAS

A rriving in the centre of town Lofty elects to do the washing whilst Tezza goes off to find them some coffee and a sticky bun as he called them.

Entering the shop with rows of washing machines and dryers, Lofty dumps his garbage bags full of dirty clothes into the largest machine he could find and pushes some buttons before wearily sitting down to wait.

The place was empty so he decided to drop the shorts he was wearing into the wash and wait till the clean ones were finished while he had a little nap.

Dozing off in his underwear near the front of the place he fails to be aware of people stopping to look in the window and laugh.

Tezza returns with the coffee wondering where Lofty has gone. Spotting a small crowd outside the Appliance Shop he wanders down to see what was going on.

It didn't take long to see what was attracting their attention. An elderly man was sitting in the front of a line of washing machines in the appliance store window in his underwear snoring his head off. It was clear to Tezza it was Lofty. The bloody idiot thought the appliance store was a laundromat and had plonked all their clothes into a dormant display model washing machine.

It was too late to save him as the police came with a distraught sales lady pointing out the situation and Lofty being led away. Fearful of being dragged into it Tezza decided to leave their clothes where they were and concentrate on getting Lofty back.

It took some doing and explaining that Lofty was a bit demented and short sighted and offering to pay for any damages that the police and the store owner decided to drop charges and let Lofty go. Hurrying out of the police station with Lofty in prison overall and protesting about false arrest and police brutality as they went, he bundled Lofty into the car and sped off.

A quick stop in the back street gave Lofty a change out of prison overalls from the remaining clothes in his suitcase and they headed off to the next town minus the clothes that Lofty left in the display washing machine.

Arriving in the centre of the next town it becomes apparent that Lofty's fame had been recognised on the afternoon news playing in the café they stopped at.

The newscaster explained.

"In local news today, an elderly man was seen in his underwear sitting inside an appliance store asleep. It appears the elderly man mistook the appliance store for a laundry mat and had piled all his dirty clothes into a new washing machine before police arrived and led the man away"

The report had several photos of Lofty being led away in his undies protesting.

Some of the café patrons noticed Lofty and identified him as the man in questions.

"Way to go Pop" said one lady

"We know where to get a cheap washing machine now pops" said her friend.

Hustling Lofty out of the café with his coffee spilling everywhere Tezza bundles Lofty into the car.

"Looks like your fame has spread around these parts Lofty. I guess flashing your parts around the appliance shop with gay abandon was all part of your 15 minutes of fame?" says Tezza.

"I'm sorry mate, perhaps its best we get out of here" says Lofty

The car sped off down the road to the highway as Lofty scanned the map for another town where they could buy some clothes to replace the ones he left in the washing machine.

Heading into a small inland town Tezza is questioning what Lofty has chosen to wear from his case, Tezza feels compelled to ask the question

"Lofty why is it you insist on dressing like that"

An indignant lofty exclaims "like what. What's wrong with my clobber" he says

"Mate, I have to tell you that it looks like you've just come out of a rags bin". says Tezza,

"I was wondering how you manage to hang onto all those daggy old rags you run around in mate. An indignant reply comes from Lofty.

"My clothes are fine there's nothing wrong with my clothing but just look at that daggy old flano you're wearing" he says with an disdainful look on his face

THE FLANO

"Theres nothing wrong with my flano's say Lofty, I've got one for every day of the week and a change for each season."

"Mate, this is me you're talking to That thing you're wearing has been with you since the 60's. How the hell do you get away with that? My missus would have chopped it up a long time ago and made me buy new stuff." says, Tezza.

"Yes, we've heard how effective that works with your gear" says Lofty smirking at Tezza in the rear-view mirror

(To those readers who are wondering what a 'Flano' is, let me enlighten you. The rest of you can skip this bit. A Flano is a term of endearment for a piece of traditional Australian Clothing, the Flannelette Shirt. Although most of these elegant pieces of attire are worn by men there are quite a few a ladys who are keen on sporting this garb from time to time. The Flano, as we shall call it from here on out, can broadly be described as a checked shirt made of flannelette. The origin of these pieces of clothing is somewhat of a mystery but they hail from the Canadian lumberjacks who wanted warm and sturdy shirts to go forth and chop down forests. Australian men seemed to have picked up the trend in the 60's or early 70's and they have been a blot on our sartorial elegance ever since according to the local fashionistas, many wives, and girlfriends)

"Tezza, I'm not here to defend the flano, or promote its wearing; it's a kind of personal man thing for me. says Lofty with a semi serious look on his face

"However, if the missus didn't like me in a flano, too bad, get over it, the flano is my territory and I feel secure wearing my flano around town. You've got to understand the power of the flano Tezza, the humble flano carries its fashion credibility cost wise and for its functionality.

"Mate, now I know you're off your rocker" says, Tezza. Bloody flano's are a useless bit of kit.

"Hold on Tezza, those girlie sports shirts you wear cannot compare to my flano's that serve a number of purposes as well as keeping me warm," says Lofty with a flourish.

"Ok go on, convince me" says Tezza with his eyes skyward.

Continuing his explanation, Lofty makes his points.

"Most flanos have 2 pockets which are nice and deep. These are great for the TAB and betting tickets. A packet of smokes fits nicely into either one or there's even room for your lighter as well.

"You can pop the odd screw and nail in there without worrying about the damage. However, old flano's are better than the new ones for that stuff. Buttons on the old flanos are strong and the flap keeps stuff from falling out."

"Beam me up Scotty; I've got a Flano connoisseur on my hands says," Tezza.

Not stopping his dialogue, Lofty continues.

"Flano's can be worn in or out of your pants and there are even nice thick ones to keep out the winter chills that act like a kind of wind cheater."

"Hold it right there Lofty, any good quality shirt can do that. says Tezza holding up a hand

"True but there is a side to the good old flano you might not have understood. It's not the colour or the pattern or even the pockets that attract me to the good old flano. It's not even the style that has me going or the fashion statement they make." says Lofty

"Style, fashion statement, you've got to be kidding mate" exclaims Lofty

"No, the main reason I love to wear them is it's the attitude they project. "

"More like BO I reckon, when did you last wash that thing anyway "says, Tezza.

Not to be put off Lofty continues his diatribe,

"Next time you see a bloke like me fronting around in his flano; before you criticize him, check out his posture. He looks taller and meaner, doesn't he? The humble flano is a transformer for most men, even you Tezza".

"Pass me that plastic bag, I think I'm gonna throw up" says Tezza making retching sounds.

"Its true mate, even the mild-mannered bank clerk during the week turns into a raging, macho handyman on the weekend when he pops into his flano on Saturday morning to mow the lawn. The young guys wear them around their waist as a kind of sexual bandana which is designed to lead the female of the species toward their nether regions." says Lofty

Tezza chimes in,

"Maybe it's just that their upper regions aren't worth looking at or that they need to hide their spreading waistlines. Tezza says pointing to Lofty's girth

Lofty continues with a look of disdain on his face

"The flano is ageless and I will continue to wear one regardless of my age.

Laughing out loud Tezza makes a point

"Mate, that thing smells like you've been buried in it already"

With a flourish of the hands in an academic gesture Lofty says,

"So what is it that drives some males toward these things. Sociologists think that they are a mark of status in a community. The flano worn at certain functions denotes a sort of class statement. 'I'm a flano man and you can all go jump' is what the wearer is saying. In other situations, the statement is one of macho dominance. 'I'm a worker and just you remember it' is what some men are saying when they parade their flanos in certain company."

"So what statement is your flano making, I'm a stinky old bloke with no fashion sense who finds his clothes in a clothing bin." says Tezza

"Your most unkind" says Lofty with a false look of hurt on his face.

Taking control of the discussion Tezza forces his points.

"if you need a shirt to show your masculinity you're missing the whole ball game. The guys that need clothing to prove their masculinity are usually trying too hard and often come off worse in the company of new age males in pink shirts.

"Women seem to relate better to metrosexuals these days, or perhaps it's the display of tattoos just below the rolled up cuffs and the problem they have with shaving that turns them on."

Looking disgusted, Lofty takes back the lead.

"if I might continue my dissertation on Flano wearing" says Lofty with a dismissive wave of his hand.

"I take your point Mr fashionista but let me give you the reasons behind certain Flano wearing styles. says Lofty looking over the top of his sunglasses.

"We have the unsure flano wearer. This person will put a tee shirt underneath his flano and leave it open to the waist with the sleeves rolled up. We're not sure what this says about the wearer but he isn't a true believer in the power of the flano.

"Then, of course, you can always buy the pre-fitted flano with imbedded T-shirt. They really don't cut the mustard with me so never buy them for your genuine flano devotee.

"Wearing one knotted around your waist is also for girly boys who aren't sure what they want or just want to hide something.

"My flano's have a special place to live as I know they would be thrown out if I left them in the wardrobe." says Lofty

"That sounds like a positive step" says, Tezza

Not to be put off, Lofty continues,

"You need to understand Flano's deserve a special place to live where they feel at home. The workshop or shed is the place to keep your favourite flano's. They love the smell of oil and stuff"

"Have you been taking your tablets mate" says Tezza with a false sense of anxiousness on his face?

"I know you're secretly a Flano man Tezza but you just haven't come out yet. Here's a tip, buy a couple of flanos to leave around the house so the wife can find them and cut them up for rags. Then make sure you protest loudly so she feels a sense of victory over the flano destruction. Always wear the shirt 'she' has bought for your birthday down to the shed but never get it dirty.

"Always wear your flano to the hardware shop. Stick a carpenter's pencil in the pocket or better still behind your ear, and shop with purpose. The flano will attract meandering females looking for solutions and they will see you as a source of knowledge. However, don't expect any of the store staff to attend to you as they figure you know what you're doing. One glance and they think 'Oh yes a flano man no need to help him. There's a tailored polo shirt guy, he'll need help"

"Okay I know you're a genius but I think you spend too much time thinking about this stuff" say, Tezza

Not to be put off, Lofty continues his lecture on Flanos.

"Flanos at a formal function can be a bit difficult to pull off. I once attended the wedding of a plumber friend's daughter who lives in his flano. He wore his to the wedding despite strong opposition from the family. However, in deference to the occasion, he did up his top button and hung a sink plug chain around his neck and flower in his buttoned-down pocket."

"Now I know you're kidding I know who you're talking about and his wife would not put up with that" says, Tezza

"Your partly right, understandably he was made to put on a dinner jacket, but it didn't really detract from the Flano. Says Lofty with a concerned look on his face

Laughter breaks out as the pair share the visual thought of their plumber mate in a flano and dinner jacket with the sink plug around his neck.

Not content that he has covered the subject fully Lofty continues.

"You must guard your flano's as women sometimes take it upon themselves to pinch them. Exactly why this is done remains a mystery, but some women claim it's done to attract their man's attention. When the ladies wear your flano without anything else on it can be a distraction but after the fun and games make sure you get your flano back as it might be a ploy to get it away from you." Says Lofty with a serious look fading on his face

More laughter ensues as Tezza decides that the madness has gone on long enough and concludes the discussion.

"So in your warped mind, the humble flano is not just a fashion statement, it's not just a style or even a personal statement. It's an attitude, it's about how we feel at the time we wear it and the reason we wear it. In time ladies learn to love the flano wearing man and won't cut up his favourite piece of kit if he is careful about its storage, right" says Tezza with a wave of his hand's indication that's the end of the discussion.

"Spot on chief "says Lofty

TEZZA'S FASHION EXPERIMENT

Not long after the marathon Flano session they pull into a nice seaside tourist town with Tezza pointing out the obvious.

"Since you threw away most of my clothes in the washing machine appliance shop, I'm going to need to buy some new stuff. You can sit here or do something else I don't care. I'm off to do some shopping" says Tezza with a look of defiance on his face as he slams the car door. Leaning back into the car Tezza suggests that Lofty might consider doing the same but not with him.

Sometime later Tezza returns to find Lofty sitting in a sidewalk café talking with locals and enjoying a coffee. Seeing Tezza approaching with a strange step in his walk, the locals leave Lofty bidding him goodbye.

"Hey mate, my fame has spread to this town and everyone is talking about Undies man. That lot wanted my autograph, no kidding. So, what happened to you and why are you walking funny asks Lofty

"It's a long story mate but get me a coffee as I can't sit down in these bloody jeans and I will tell you all about my adventure in the car" says Tezza grimacing as he sits down awkwardly in the passengers seat whilst Lofty gets the coffees.

Coffee in hand Tezza begins the story

"You know my wardrobe is a bit old so I figured I might tidy it up with some new stuff. I also recognized that perhaps my Tee shirt wearing days were over. I'm not into tight jeans but I thought it was time to get a pair that didn't look like they were made for miners during the Gold Rush."

"No never" says Lofty smirking at his mates' obvious admissions about his dress sense.

"Ok, I'm not a fashion plate like you Mr Flano but I found a trendy shop with music (I use the term lightly) blaring out and confronted the disinterested young girl behind the counter to get some help. I got the piss off I'm busy texting look. She did point to the back corner of the shop as it was no use trying to yell over the raucous noise masquerading as music."

"I know what you mean go on this scenario sounds a bit like one of my episodes". says Lofty,

"Well, The jeans I found appeared to have 3 sizes on the label which left me confused. Thus, I picked what looked like a pair that might fit and after embarrassing myself by trying to get into a booth occupied by a half-dressed young woman trying on a bikini, I stumbled into a booth and struggled on with the jeans. The fit wasn't bad but as usual, my sensible undies let me down as the wedding tackle got tangled in the zip."

"Must have been tight to catch your willy" says Lofty giggling

Tezza frowns but continues.

"Anyway, I struggled out to the front counter asking the young thing behind the counter if she could help me whilst yanking at my crotch. The police quite understood and let me go with a warning after helping me sort out the offending jeans and made me pay for the wretched things, laughing as they did so. Have you seen the price of this stuff? Could have bought a year's worth of No 8s (navy work clothes before camo came in) for that rip-off."

"Judging by your attire I thought you had", smirks Lofty

Tezza continues,

"Why is it that my wedding tackle seems to be living a life of its own these days. It doesn't work very well anymore but it never stops trying to embarrass me these days."

"Anyway, in my effort to find equilibrium between extrovert and introvert I decided a nice new pair of loafers (the modern name for up market sandshoes) would be a deal changer to wear with my new jeans that don't fit.

"Here we go again I can sense another disaster coming" says, Lofty.

"Well, I went to the shoe shop in my shorts as the jeans were unwearable. I was busy trying on various pairs of loafers when I noticed the sales lady talking to the store security guy and pointing in my direction." Says Tezza

"So, what had you done this time, made rude noises, farted loudly??" says Lofty,

"No, my sensible undies let me down again as it appears the old fella had been making a regular appearance from under the leg of my shorts as I tried on the shoes. I got off with a warning again but the cops made me put the jeans on before I left the store. I won't wear those shorts in public again but these bloody jeans are killing me. I paid for the last pair of loafers I tried on which were iridescent blue as you can see and didn't fit but I wasn't going to hang about with everybody looking at me and giggling.".

"Must have been very short shorts ole mate," says Lofty with a wry giggle

"It wasn't over yet. I'm wearing my ill-fitting jeans and blue loafers that don't fit either but like a fool I decided a haircut was necessary to set off the new look. Normally I go to a male barber and discuss men stuff. However, I decided on this occasion to go to the hairdresser near the shoe shop in the mall to escape the giggles and titters that seemed to follow me up the mall."

"Geez, I wonder why" says Lofty gazing skyward.

"Well, it turned out to be one of those overpriced hair stylists that always seems to smell like somebody set fire to an old mattress or lounge suite. The young hairdresser lady sits me down and puts a scented drape over me from neck to knee. After snipping and fluffing around, I thought I might clean my glasses under the drape before looking at what she had done to my hair, or the lack of it." says Tezza with a hang dog expression on his face

"Now I know your bullshitting mate, those drapes are long, there's no way your", Tezza cuts off Lofty mid-sentence

"Mate all I remember is being hit over the back of the head and called a dirty old man before being thrown into the mall with half a haircut. It appears the hairdresser lady thought the cleaning I was giving my glasses was mistaken for rubbing something else under the drape."

"I can guess how that would be the case you ole wanker" says Lofty, giggling

"I did try to explain but they didn't believe me.

"So, what's the tally" says, Lofty?

"In my effort to find equilibrium in old age I've pissed off most of the locals, upset shop assistants and hairdressers and all I can show for it are a pair of ill-fitting jeans, blue ill-fitting sandshoes and half-finished $60 haircut. Oh yes almost forgot, I'm on the local plods watch list now with you from your escapade in the appliance shop."

"I think it would have been easier for you to have stayed a worn-out fashionista." says Lofty

"Perhaps it's time we got back to the job at hand and continue the road trip"says Tezza

Agreeing it was time to leave when they saw the local police car cruising past and looking in their direction, they back out and head off down a nearby laneway to find an escape route. It wasn't long before they were back on the highway leaving the town far behind but the reputations following them

------*ele*------

Tezza had commandeered the CD player and was lost in the world of Petula Clark, The Shadows and Johnny Mathis, when Lofty comments,

"Mate I am sure we are identical twins but separated at birth. The music you selected is fabulous right up my alley, is there anything that one of us likes and the other dislikes,"

"Not that I can think of it is a wonder we never married twins to complete the set. says Tezza continuing his thoughts

"We came close mate if you recall how that all played out" says Tezza reflecting on the times they had met the nurses from a local hospital.

"I remember shopping in London in 67 when we were on the lookout for a three-quarter warm coats, we found a shop with reasonable prices. They had a style and price that suited us, Ten Quid I think, that was the top of our price range so in reality we should not have been in there, luckily it was on special and apparently if not sold it was destined for the rags old bag on any submarine that needed it. That sale had good and bad attached to it, the good being the price, the bad was that they had only two left and they were identical,

"Your comment as I recall mate was, we will look like the Bobbsey Twins, bugger it what the heck better than being cold, I suppose the hope was maybe wearing them would attract the other pair of female Bobbsey Twins, but of course despite wearing them to death it never happened," says Tezza

Smiling, Lofty cut in

"So what's new."

Tezza continues,

"So, twins get a zero, did you ever score a mother and Daughter act Lofty,"

"Tezza what have you been smoking, no, I am going to the big home in the sky with no points in that category, what about you Tezza," says Lofty

"No stories to report on that score. Although as you may recall we came close in Holland with the two girls we met on the ferry.

The discussions around that little adventure flowed back and forth for some time as it was a very happy memory for both men.

With some driving behind them they were approaching a Celtic type of town that Lofty had been to before. Lofty says,

"I will drive you around a bit as this is a lovely little town but be warned I think they export families to Tasmania to keep the inbreeding program alive down there. So don't cross swords with anyone here as the outcome is very unpredictable." Says Lofty with a naughty smile on his face

The boys drove around for a while before arriving in a high-altitude park and taking in the view of the town.

"Surely the people living in this picturesque town must be contented with their lot" says Tezza.

"Not sure of that, would be a pain in the arse when everyone in town is likely to be your relative. Also makes for some confusion on fathers' day. Anyway it's time to eat". says Lofty

"What else, but I agree I am a bit hungry. says Tezza

Leaving the park behind and heading into the Town center Lofty was surprised to see that a police car had settled in behind them and was indicating they wanted to have a word with the driver. Lofty pulled over and was approached by a 5 foot nothing policewoman, Tezza commented

"I wonder what the cops want with us, you certainly did not appear to be breaking any laws,"

"Don't forget where we are." Lofty commented

A young policewoman approached the driver's window

"Good morning, Sir, may I see your licence," she said.

"Did I do something wrong Maam," says Lofty?

The height challenged policewoman gets irate,

"Sir I will ask the questions, and I would be pleased if you addressed me as an Officer Candy thank you!"

"No problem, Officer Candy. I bet you come from a long line of grateful people with a surname like that" say Lofty.

Seeing steam coming out of her ears and noting the policewoman was sporting the rank of Senior Constable, Lofty decided to apologise and stir the irate policewoman up a bit.

"Constable Randy we have already had a poor day for two old blokes, so please be gentle with us."

"I'm a senior constable, and my name is Candy please remember that when you address me sir".

Lofty of course knew exactly what she was about but was not going to be beaten by some uniformed little girl who in his days would have been indoctrinating children on the dangers of talking to strangers, taking care that she finished in time to get back to the station to wash the cups and prepare for the change of shifts at 3 o'clock.

"Your licence seems to be in order sir, have you consumed alcohol within the last 24 hours" The Police person asks

"Look corporal, weve had a hard 24 hours and"

before he had gone any further, The young Police person shouts.

"Ok that's it, step out of the vehicle please Sir,"

Standing on the gutter to raise her height somewhat the lady cop says.

"let's get one thing straight, I am a Senior Constable in the Police, right"

Lofty thought to himself, tempting though it may be don't go any further or this little piece could lock us up and feed us to the arse plugging banjo set in her jail. Tezza meanwhile had got out of the vehicle and stood around the other side.

By now the policewoman's partner was making her way towards Lofty and Tezza. This member of the Constabulary was also a female, Lofty mumbled something inaudible. The second cop was in her late twenties with a face like a smacked arse and nose hair like barbed wire.

However, this harbinger of doom was sporting silver scrambled egg on her hat. Lofty and Tezza looked at each other and the look told the story, not a word would be said they were on a non-winner here and in this situation it's best not to inflame the situation any further. After all, wasn't it just a few days ago Lofty was an overnight guest of the Government and that was probably on the record these two could look up and probably had already.

"Sir the reason I pulled you up is that your vehicle crossed over double lines, do you have any reason for this,

Turning to Tezza she says in a not too friendly manner,

"Sir get back into the vehicle please."

"Double lines what blo---, Lofty withheld his tongue,

"Officer's, I understand that there is no way to refute your accusation so if you would please give me the ticket we will leave this money-making locality and head North where people are, sens"--- again he bit his tongue.

The senior one of the pair now wanted her two bobs worth,

"Sir due to your obvious City attitude, leading to contempt, I am considering whether to charge you with offensive behavior," she says

It was now where Lofty realised why Tezza was smarter than he. Hearing all this Tezza got out of the car and approached the trio.

"Excuse me officers may I say something that may save a lot of paperwork and any further angst, I am travelling with my alleged accused friend here and I have overheard all the conversations thus far. I am not saying whether any guilt is attached to my friend here or not but looking at the footage on our rear-view dash cam I do find it curious that neither of you are wearing your protective high visibility vests, and I am aware that this is a breach of policy guidelines having spent some time in that area." Tezza says with a studied look on his face like a lawyer at a trial.

Both Officers glared at Tezza and if hate could be transferred via the eyes Tezza was in deep shit. After a quick and private conversation, the pair of Officer's came back. Speaking to Lofty the senior of the two stated that the road offence will be overlooked as a minor breach of the Law and no further action will be taken, however, you are advised to continue your journey immediately with no further stops in our town, we will be enforcing this request, I believe you can read the undercurrent of this request, here is your licence, good morning gentlemen.

Back in the car with Tezza now at the wheel, the pair head off out of town with the police car following them to the outer limits before turning back. Lofty was beaming from ear to ear,

"How did you pull that one out of your hat mate, we don't have a rear dash cam."

"You forget Lofty part of my service life was in Naval Police, and they could neither confirm or deny that the little reversing camera this thing has didn't have them on record."

"Well done old son that's one I owe you,"

"No mate that's another one you owe me, Lofty I think I must agree somewhat with the Feds, I think you have an attitude problem, you were brave but stupid to push it with those two.

"Mate if one of those two had been an old time Crown Sergeant, you and I would not be having this conversation due to the fact blood that would be streaming from our mouth and possibly our arse as well." says Tezza

"You are so right Tezza, anyway as hungry as I am I think we should take the win and find the next town for something to eat, hopefully, it won't be near this bloody place, I told you they were inbred,

"You also told me to watch my step, what happened Nostradamus" Tezza says laughing out loud,

"You always must have the last say don't you, don't be cruel and drive on oh brave and fearless Tour Leader, drive on, says Lofty with a flourish like a knight on a charging horse.

DRIVER OBSERVATIONS

Having escaped the tyranny of the regional town, Tezza and Lofty had time to reflect on the idiosyncratic behavior of drivers in traffic congestion. Observing the habits and behavior of fellow traffic jammers had become a bit of a pastime for Lofty and helped him pass the time and lessen the stress of being late and wasting time and fuel.

Tezza had found there was a distinct correlation between the vehicle and the person and went on to explain his thoughts:

The discussion flowed and helped them pass the time with meaningless banter and thoughts.

"The large and intimidating pickup truck drivers have urban cowboy attitudes with bulls horns on the back window although judging by the immaculately clean state their vehicles the biggest adventure they had seen was a McStodges drive through." says Lofty who saw them as a particular breed

"Agreed, then there is the BMW and Mercedes set. They varied quite a bit but all exuded an air of self-importance and entitlement as they wafted along." says Tezza.

"Okay but let's not forget the middle age hoon in their sports cars of many varieties. They can be seen ducking and diving in and out of lanes to show how adept they are and why a Ferrari scout should book them for the next formula one Grand Prix. says Lofty

"Let's not forget the young females. They love to prove that you are the glass ceiling and demand you get out of their way to the top by tailgating as close as possible." Says Tezza

Lofty then commented that he often observed what he called adventure man. These folk usually have urban 4x4's with all the trimmings. They sit high above the traffic snarl and gives off the air of crocodile Dundee while monstering as many helpless smaller cars as they can on their way to filling up 2 car spaces in the car park.

"Van boys are the next interesting category. They don't give a shit. It's not their van and they get paid regardless so you will see them passing by with passengers' feet on the dash or out the window eating a burger or trying to tailgate the beamer with a little blonde unit in it or ogling the passing female pedestrian traffic." says Tezza

"Okay, that's another world problem solved. Maybe special licences should be granted to these special people. In fact, it's typical to drop your Beamer of Merc key on the bar to impress the ladies, so maybe that's the symbolism needed" says Lofty

"Yeh but Im not sure a set of Toyota keys would produce the same effect. I had a mate who restored a BMW Isetta 3 wheeler. You may recall its the one with the front opening door and the wheel at the back that had room for only two people. He had a set of keys with gold embellishment on them and he loved to drop them on the bar. You can imagine the look he got when he pulled a lady.

Both laugh at the image of Tezza's friend and his little 3 wheeler deciding they should stop and get some fuel for the car and themselves they pull into a remote service station off the freeway for a rather large shake and fruit juice.

THE DOLPHIN TORCH URINAL

After swapping drivers and with Lofty back at the wheel they head off back onto the highway and a short time later hit a traffic jam and could see no end in sight. As time passed and with their bladders full and no suitable place to pull over and relieve themselves things were getting desperate.

Fearing that if they pulled into the breakdown lane and took a piss the cameras would catch them and a fine or worse would ensue.

"Mate, I've got to take a piss or I'm going to burst" says Tezza

"Me too chief, not a problem. Reach over the back and grab those two dolphin torches" says Lofty

Fumbling around the back seat as the car slowly crawls along in the traffic, Tezza finds the two large dolphin torches behind his seat. These large plastic lantern style torches had been brought with them in case of a breakdown and for night time stops.

"Listen, I need to urinate not illuminate the problem " says Tezza putting the two torches on his lap.

"So, what am I supposed to do with these" asks Tezza?

He didn't have to wait long as Lofty gave him a practical demonstration by removing the lens part and the battery and filling the body of the torch with piss.

"What the fuck are you doing" says Tezza as Lofty finishes and shakes the remnants around the cabin.

"See, this is how you do it. Happens regularly with the Missus and me and these wonderful torches hold a suitable amount of piss and are waterproof from both sides." Says Lofty

"Mate your full of surprises aren't you, I would pay to see you guys pissing into a torch in the car, where did you learn that trick" enquires Tezza.

"Well Lofty if you spend a few hours on the road or in the air and can't leave or get up to piss you learn to improvise." Says Lofty

"Ok, I get the picture."says Tezza

With that it was off with the top and away went Tezza into his torch body (with the battery removed of course). However, the pair soon discovered that with two full torch bodies now in Tezza's hands in the passenger seat it was impossible to screw the lens parts back on and seal the container despite trying to and spilling the piss on the seat and floor.

"Now what are we going to do genius" says Tezza with his lap soaked with piss.

"Easy mate, as we are in the left lane you can dump the contents overboard through your half open window." says Lofty,

"Ok chief, but remember that I have a torch body full of piss in each hand so you will have to lower my window with your controls." Says Tezza trying to not spill anymore

"Okay mate but be bloody careful as we don't want the car to smell like a dunny right!" says Lofty triggering the passenger window switch.

Tezza wrestles with his seat belt and in so doing manages to spill more of the contents of the torch bodies. With the window down both temporary urinals are emptied out of the window and onto the breakdown lane. Good plan and it did work with one small catch.

An inpatient BMW convertible caught in the traffic jam flashes up the breakdown lane with its top down (as you do on every occasion above freezing point if you own a convertible).

A semi balding, wig wearing driver with his blonde trophy partner beside him decided they had enough of sitting in the traffic or perhaps he was on a promise and decided to chance his hand by running up the breakdown lane at a fair clip to get to the next exit around the bend.

Unfortunately, the BMW arrived alongside the lad's car at the very moment the urinal dump was in progress and was perfectly timed so they copped the lot. Going at quite a pace the BMW convertible disappeared around the corner and smashed into the back of the highway patrol car that was clearing up the accident that had caused all the delays.

As they approach the scene of the accident with the BMW firmly parked in the boot of the highway patrol car Tezza is the first to speak

"Shit now were in trouble. That looks like the same policewomen that pulled us over in town."

Sinking low in their seats as they pass the scene, they notice the BMW drivers poorly fitting wig had detached itself from his head (maybe piss melts wig glue? Thinks Lofty.) His girlfriend had her hair matted to her head and makeup running down her face and is battering Mr. BMW with her handbag from one side whilst the policewoman from town writes him what must have been a not inconsiderable ticket on the other side. Fortunately, that meant she had her back to the lads as they passed

Passing the damaged squad car with the BMW firmly planted in its boot, Lofty comments

"Mate, I have a feeling we ruined Mr. BMW's dirty weekend and our lady cop's day."

convinced they were clear of any reprimand Tezza sits upright and speaks

"I think the BMW driver was a little pissed off Lofty." With a smirk on his face

"That's an understatement Tezza. At least that puts a new meaning to being on the piss" says Lofty, and the pair burst in raucous laughter.

After a brief stop and munching on bacon and egg rolls, the pair heads into a section of narrow roads and long flat paddocks full of sugar cane. Tezza sees a tanker truck plodding along in front of them and wonders about the chances of passing it with random traffic coming the other way.

"Just what we need mate, a bloody tanker on a slow section of road. He will be hard to pass" says Lofty from the driver's seat.

MR WHIFFY

As they get closer Tezza notices the tanker is leaking.

"We need to get around this guy and let him know he is leaking.

The closer they get the more substantial the leak appears on the tanker and the windscreen gets dirtier by the minute from the leak splashing back at them. Hanging out the window Lofty is trying to see a clear space for overtaking but the traffic is sporadic and frustrating.

"I don't know what this guy's hauling but it stinks" says Lofty as the leaking substances hits the road and splashes back onto the car and them with greater volume as they get closer.

Finally seeing a clear stretch Lofty floors it and they head out on the wrong side of the road to pass the truck with windscreen wipers flat out and Lofty hanging out the window and covered in the stuff leaking out of the tanker.

As they pass the truck's cab, Tezza signals to the tanker driver that he is leaking, and the driver acknowledges but keeps going.

"Never heard of that fuel mob Lofty", says Tezza who is also now covered in the leaking material having opened his window before they overtook the tanker.

"What was the name on the tankerTezza?" Says Lofty trying to clear his windscreen and wipe some of the stuff off his face

"Mr. Whiffy, I think." says Tezza looking for something to wipe his face with

"Shit that was a sewerage pump out truck." says Lofty

"So that means we are covered in……."

"Exactly old mate... Shit." Says Lofty

Tezza vomits into the foot well adding to the odor of spilt piss and old food and now sewerage.

"Oh, great, now we have the trifecta. the car and both of us are covered in shit, you've vomited all over the place and I've just pissed myself again" says Lofty

"Better pull over and try to clean us and the car up" says Tezza.

"No way mate. If we stop that tanker will come past us again and we will be right back where we started. There's a town about 80kms up the road and I'll wager that's where the tanker was heading and where we should stop and clean up." says Lofty

The day was hot and humid and the smell in the car they decided to drive with the windows open. It took over an hour to reach the next town. The deluge of stuff in the car and on each of them had dried to a kind of stinking crust as they pulled into the first service station they came across. They parked near the water and air station and stripped down to their undies so they could hose each other down. It wasn't long before a police car pulls up next to them and the local cop strolls over.

"Afternoon fellas, what do you think you're doing?" he asks

"Officer, we were following a tanker which was leaking shit, and it got all over us" says Tezza scraping at the crusty shit on his legs.

The police officer is not amused and lets them know in no uncertain terms.

"Fellas, stop playing with the water hose, get your gear on and get out of here. That's a girl's school across the road if you hadn't noticed and the headmistress phoned us to tell us there were two old men flashing their parts at the girls and playing with the garage hose.

"I've checked you out and there's a record of a discussion you had in the last town you stopped at and some suspicion you may have been involved in an accident on the Freeway involving a BMW and a patrol car. Now get out of here before I arrest you both."

The pair quickly jump back into the car with just there undies on and head out of town toward the highway just in time to see Mr Whiffy flash past. It was not a good afternoon, and the pair spent the night beside a creek after being thrown out of a motel as a pair of perverts who arrived at reception in their underwear and stinking of shit.

The following morning was bright and clear, and the pair had managed to clean themselves up somewhat in the park lake before heading out but the car was a mess and stunk to high heaven.

"Not far to go now mate" says Tezza looking at the map.

"Yeh, we are only 2 days late but that's OK, you can talk us out of this can't you Tezza." says Lofty grinning with the remnants of yesterdays shit storm still in his hair.

"I will try but this car is something else." Says Tezza

"Maybe we should take a present to the ladies to smooth things out" says Lofty.

It sounded like a plan but they decided to find a truck stop somewhere so they could have a shower and try and clean up the car a little. An hour later they pulled into a big truck stop known as 'Big Trucker' that many had called something else because of the prostitutes that hung around the place looking for business in the truck sleeper cabs.

After hosing out the floor of the car with a pressure washer hose they headed for the showers and cleaned themselves up to a reasonable standard before heading back to the road and the final stages of their journey. Along the way they decided it would be a good idea to pick up some food and groceries maybe as the hotel they had booked them into had small kitchen facilities. They figured this would save them a few dollars in meals whilst they were there.

THE FOOD RUN

A few km's down the road they saw a sign for a major supermarket in the town at the end of the turn off. Tezza swung the car into the exit lane and nudging Lofty who had dozed off he said

"Mate as discussed, we should stop and pick up some supplies before we catch up with the ladies. Theres a supermarket here" says Tezza.

Lofty looks over the top of his sunnies and says,

"Are you fucking mad, don't you know what day it is?"

Tezza responds curtly,

"yeh mate I'm not senile yet, it's Thursday"

"No fool, its pension day" says Lofty

"So what "says Tezza with a questioning look on his face

"Mate, everybody knows that despite everything being plentiful in this country, most pensioners are all out and about. stocking up with enough to last for a trip to Mars and back on pension day. If you've never had the displeasure of having to shop on pension day then you're in for a hell of a shock and you're on your own" says Lofty

"Regardless of your fears we agreed we needed a few things from a supermarket but I can't do it on my own!" says Tezza

Loftys response and horror at the thought was immediate and to the point.

"Are you @#^$&% mad..... Its pension day... pension day"

Tezza's look confirms there is no alternative. It's shopping or copping a pizzling from the women for letting Tezza loose in a supermarket if he doesn't obey. Thinks Lofty.

The debate continues as, they head off into the jaws of hell. Tezza manages to survive the Kamikaze drivers and pensioner parking comedies all mixed with the usual pension day spirit of ill will and aggression. There are 2 old ladies fighting over a shopping trolley that someone has carefully left in a parking space whilst 2 younger men shape up for a fight over a parking space, all backed by a cacophony of car horns, squealing tyres and duff duff music from one car that seems to be intent on entertaining the whole car park with his brand of music (if that's what it was).

Meanwhile, Tezza is getting a shopping list together whilst parking and offering driving tips as the chaos around them continues.

They managed to park and fight their way to the shopping mall to be harassed by the usual lottery ticket and raffle commandos who know exactly when to strike. But Tezza's secret weapon is brought into play as Tezza has a firm grip of Loftys arm and brushes them aside like a well-trained Ninja. Pity about that, says Lofty looking back over his shoulder

"I might have feigned interest in looking at that new BMW that the pretty young thing in a short dress was promoting. Maybe on the way out Tezza, then again ambition always exceeds capability I guess" says Lofty being dragged along.

Moving on toward their objective, Lofty notices a slightly disheveled fat guy in a clown suit swaying gentle in the overpowering breeze created by the air conditioning near the midway. A feeble laugh issues forth from the obviously disgruntled fat guy in the faded red suit selling some crap by doing tricks with balloons that look like giant dicks.

"Hi kids" came the greeting from the clown person to passing masses. A pair of little kids in brightly coloured ill-fitting shorts issue a return greeting

"Piss off Fatso" the little darlings spit out as they pass.

Whack! followed by howls of distress come from the little darling as his overweight mother in exercise pants clouts him over the back of his head.

"How many times I gotta tell ya, that's ya Uncle Billy so mind ya F#@#ing language. Kid looks up quizzically at the muffin topped, tattooed beauty he calls mum and says,

"How many F@#$ing Uncles have I got, stuff the old fat bastard"

Whack, another yowl and the pair disappear into the maelstrom of desperados searching for a trolley.

"Hey Tezza; I wonder whether that kid has brain damage from all the whacks he must have received in his short lifetime. Says Lofty noticing the Tezza has become distracted in his fight for a trolley and one for Lofty

After short circuiting the trolley fight by intercepting the harassed trolley boy as he emerges out of his bat cave at the entrance to the supermarket the pair battle their way past two oldies who have decided to discuss their life's work in the middle of the entrance until one is taken out by the brain damaged kid using a trolley as a skateboard.

Whack, another correction from muffin top Mum and the entrance is cleared.

"Welcome to Stodgealways the finest food people" Blasts out of the crackling PA with a background of suitably modified elevator songs specially modified to suit the store. Must have taken days to turn Danny boy into san Choy bow and tripe, thinks Lofty

' Oh san choy bow the tripe tripe the tripe is filling' goes the song. Lofty can think of a few Scots that would turn in their grave if they heard it but at least one old fart is whistling along with it.

Lofty finds himself happily humming along with the boy band when suddenly, he's on the floor. His legs taken out from under him by a trolley wielding middle aged woman sneering at him indignantly.

"Well!, can you please move I need to get my potatoes" she says with a tone of authority in her voice,

Resisting the urge to deliver her potatoes to a place where the sun doesn't shine Lofty gets to his feet with a helping hand and a comforting voice from a supermarket guardian angel. Helping him over to the deli area with a quiet and comforting voice she asks if he is alright. No, it's not his guardian angel but one of supermarkets finest.

"Happens a lot this time of year. Would you like a drink and a sit-down sir " she says consoling Lofty who is taking it all in. But before Lofty can claim injury status and escape the madness to an adjacent office, Tezza arrives on the scene and hustles Lofty away explaining as they depart that he's always falling over, don't worry I've got him now, you know how these old fellas are. Bloody cheek thinks Lofty.

"Thanks, mate, says Lofty, I was onto a good thing there."

Tezza stops him mid-sentence.

"You wish, your days of storeroom sex are well past old fella. Tell you what just stand here and don't move and Ill sort out the stuff we need." Says Tezza

"I'm not going to argue about that chief "says Lofty leaning casually on the trolley.

The trolley and Lofty are parked near a stand full of salami looking stuff that smells awful. Meanwhile, Tezza does battle with a confused deli team and disabled ticket machine. This looked like sport to Lofty as one elderly lady swings a cabanossi at another younger female and exchanges harsh words about who was first. His thoughts were interrupted by a female voice.

"Excuse me, Excuse me, I need to get to the tins of goats tongues behind you" explains the pretty young thing with a basket and pointing at the cans on the bottom of an imported foods pyramid that must have taken some poor sod hours to erect.

Looks like, she is planning an interesting dinner of sorts so who am I to stand in the way. Ever the gentleman, Lofty offers to reach them for her. As Lofty reaches gingerly to extract what she wants he manages to topple the pyramid and 30 cans of assorted goat tongues, Yak meat and God knows what else, falls gracefully into his trolley.

Looking a little sheepish Lofty hand the one can, she wanted and quickly retreats to the Chicken section and burys his head in the giblets and necks section whilst a rather large disgruntled female store person berates the pretty young thing for vandalising the display.

Despite her protestation she is told to leave the store and don't come back. Strewth, these guys are serious thinks Lofty feeling bad for the pretty young thing but feeling assured that he saved some poor sod from a crappy dinner of Goats tongue flambé or something.

Tezza, looking stressed, comes around the corner and dumps and arm load of white paper wrapped things on top of the cans Lofty has just inherited and is too scared to try and put them back.

"What are you doing here, when I put you somewhere you stay put. You know how you always have problems in supermarkets according to your missus, just look at that poor girl who knocked over all the cans. So, stay put" he says as he departs for other regions.

"Yes, chief" says Lofty feigning a salute and snapping to attention, as Tezza weaves his way expertly through the throngs of locust-like shoppers struggling for the last sweet potato and celery stick.

The pace of shopping has increased as Lofty stands in his allotted place and observes the nonsense going on around him.

Pensioners are battling with each other over the pineapples in the tinned food aisle; some fatties are struggling with each other over the last tub of custard whilst some runaway kids are busy sampling everything, they can get their hands on. Oh, and there's the leader of the pack, the brain damaged kids from the entrance and fat clown incident.

The shopping horde has decided that the Chicken section is the next place to devour and Lofty is quickly surrounded by people grabbing stuff and pushing and shoving.

With pressure mounting Lofty decides to ignore Tezza's orders. I don't care what Tezza wants he thinks, I'm off to the soft drink aisle which looks relatively calm. With the skill of a rally driver, Lofty finds a space at the end of the aisle and settles back on the handles of his trolley.

Peace is short lived as a cluster of seemingly related shoppers descend on the soft drinks' aisle with a purposeful vengeance. The little darling they had seen on the way in had decided to climb on the shelves to get to his favourite brand of fruity pop stuff.

Wallop, a soft drink bottle lands on Lofties head as another 6 fall into his trolley.

That's it, I'm off to the freezer section before anything else happens thinks Lofty. So, with a trolley full of foreign canned stuff, fruity pop and deli stuff he heads toward the freezer aisle where he suspects Tezza might be found.

The milk section looks busy with people trying to get the longest used by date milk and blocking the whole aisle so it's time for a short cut. thinks Lofty

Round the pharmacy aisle he heads as a short-sighted woman dumps a big pack of feminine hygiene things into his trolley by mistake. Lofty not stopping heads off down the main aisle and into the home wares aisle which should be relatively quiet. Bosh, he is hit head on by a mobility scooter that knocks him and the trolley into the Kitty Litter display.

A bag of kitty litter has split and emptied into his trolley followed by a split bag of foul-smelling manure followed by a carton of flea powder has spilt all over the pensioner who now looks like a white Darlec off the Dr Who TV series.

With the abusive pensioner hot in pursuit, Lofty makes a sharp right turn and hides in the cosmetics section. Voices from the other side of the displays alert Lofty to the fact he is not alone.

"I'm not sure I like your new perfume" Lofty hears from the next aisle as he hides with his stinking trolley load of stuff whilst pretending to look through the foot care products. The disgruntled pensioner covered in flea powder speeds past and fails to see Lofty or the cluster of shoppers around the milk cabinets. Bang crash wallop, pensioner, milk shoppers and others all go flying. That's just the distraction Lofty needs as he heads for the nearest checkout which seems to have cleared as he heads in with his stinking trolley load.

People begin avoiding him and looking at the mess in his trolley and the trail he's left behind him. A little old lady is arguing about the price of frozen peas with an ever patient check out chick. Seeing the look of desperation in Loftys face, he is hustled through by a bemused floor manager type who informs him that he will have to pay for all the stuff in his trolley.

"Yes yes just get me out of here" Lofty exclaims as the mayhem in the milk aisle escalates with the kids knocking over the soft drink displays to get a better vantage point to view the chaos in the milk aisle. Meanwhile someone else has destroyed the foreign food display yet again. The ladies in the cosmetic section are complaining that the perfumed stuff has gone off without knowing its Lofty's trail of manure that is responsible. The young thing has returned with her partner, a man mountain Maori, who is gesturing vigorously at an intimidated waif of a boy in a supermarket apron. The trolley fight continues at the front and the fat clown is wrestling with some kid who is trying to wrench his big shoes off. Meanwhile the songs blast out of the PA to the tune of colonel bogey march

" Oh, when the washing goes marching in, Oh when the washing goes marching in. I want a box of Elmers Sudsa, when the washing goes marching in."

Lofty makes a hasty retreat toward the car park whistling the tune and wondering what he will do with all the crap in his trolley.

Tezza appears with an armful of stuff and abuses Lofty for leaving his appointed station and threatens disclosure in front of the wives. Lofty just waves and says

"See you at the car" and heads off at a brisk pace with his smelly trolley load of stuff.

Back in the relative calm of the now full car park Lofty examines his trolley load of crap. He feels a song coming on as he merrily rifles through the mess to the amusement of fellow shopper when he begins to sing to the tune of the first day of Christmas,

On the pension day at Stodgealways my true love brought to me

30 cans of goat tongues

10 cans of Mexican spam

6 half empty bottles of fruity pop

2 split and empty bottles of cherry cola

2 open bags of kitty litter

Half a bag of cat food open

1 bag open of organic horse manure which has covered everything

10 bags of deli goods soaked in fruity pop, kitty litter and horse poo

and a big expanding bag of feminine hygiene thingies

Lofty is wondering what to do with all this stuff as Tezza storms up and screams at him.

"What the hell have you bought here, and geez you stink. I hope you're not going to put all that crap in the car"

best not to argue thinks Lofty.

"So where is all my deli stuff."...... long pause as Tezza sees the congealed mess that once was leg ham and corn beef.

"I had hoped you had at least got the deli stuff safely to the car". I couldn't get any milk as there was some kind of disaster down there and the bread area was off limits as there were cans of stuff all over the floor. Let's get out of here" he says looking dejected

"I did warn you mate" says Lofty with a look of triumph.

"If I didn't know better, I would think you might have had a hand in all that" says Tezza peering inquisitively at Lofty whilst Lofty looks innocently skyward.

Trying to look sad and dejected to garner some sympathy Lofty watches as Tezza wheels the smell trolley full of stuff over towards a dumpster.

"That's the last time I'm taking you shopping" Yes! Lofty exclaims under his breath still trying to hold a sad dejected look.

"I'm going to drop you at the hotel with the ladies and see what I can find at the nearest 7 eleven". Says Tezza

Lofty thinks to himself, I guess there's always something good that comes out these things. I'm sure the feral cats had a great dinner in the Dumpster. Maybe Tezza has learnt to keep clear of shopping malls at all costs on pension days.

As they glide past the parked cars, Tezza noticed the ferals again and says,

"Oh on my way to the dumpster I managed to slip a leaking bottle of fruity pop covered in Horse poo into the feral kids' car boot when they weren't looking. I also noticed that the brain damaged kids had copped another whack around their head as they were leaving as mum was not impressed with their comments about the odor in their car. I think they deserved a helping of sticky horse poo in their boot don't you Lofty

"Right on Chief, right on" says Lofty as the pair burst into more laughter heading down the road towards their destination in their hire car still reeking of sewage, vomit and piss worse than the aft mess on a submarine after a big night ashore.

"Going to take some cleaning mate "says Tezza opening all the windows whilst looking around the car.

MOTEL BLUES

The car slid into the budget priced Shady Rest Motel car park, they had booked from home. Lofty began to unpack the car whilst Tezza went to the front desk to enquire which rooms their wives were in.

The car was a mess and stank to high heaven from all the exploits along the way. Lofty was wondering how much the hire car company would penalise them when they returned it.

Tezza as always was positive and said he had a mate with a super car wash that would have it looking like new, but Lofty was doubtful that the pungent odor from their run in with Mr. Whiffy and the piss out the window trick would ever be expunged.

Tezza returns with the news that the wives were not here but had left a note saying they have relocated to the Costa Lotta 5-star hotel near the beach. The rest of the note went on about cheap skates and not staying in a rundown flop house etc.

"Shit, that place is going to cost a bomb. Looks like it's a second mortgage for us" says Lofty.

Packing up the car, the intrepid pair head over to the swank hotel. They're greeted in the driveway by a Nigel Nice type in a bow tie and unusually white teeth strutting purposefully toward them.

"I'm sorry, but the trade's entrance for deliveries is around the back you can't come in this way" explains Nigel Nice with a polite but firm hand on the car door but turning his head away from the pungent odor emanating from the car..

"Mate; we are guests here so button your lip and show us where to park this thing". says Tezza, firmly but politely

After some back and forth and checking Nigel Nice dispatches some poor little dude to park the car whilst disdainfully motioning the lads to the reception desk.

"Not good news. The bloody women only booked one room but I've managed to get us a room in the basement. It's all they had left. It appears there's a vets convention in town." says Tezza. smiling

"Who would have guessed, okay let's get all this shit down to our room and go find the bloody wives". says Lofty,

However, an hour of searching and ringing the room fails to find the ladies. After enquiries at the concierge desk Tezza finds out they had gone whale watching. Returning to where Lofty was sitting in the bar he announces his findings

"Well mate, appears they've gone whale watching, nothing for it but to have a drink". says Tezza

"Right on but judging by what I'm seeing in the pool over yonder they could have done their whale watching here" says Lofty following Tezza into the banana bar and finding a quiet corner in which to drown their sorrows.

"Your shout" says Tezza as they pass the bar ordering 2 small beers.

"That'll be $31 please sir" said the barman.

With an indignant look and holding up his credit card Lofty sarcastically asks

"Mate, I only want to borrow the glass not buy it; it's the beer inside it that I want." He says

"Yes sir $31 is the price of 2 BEERS."

With his usual ability to get into strife it isn't long before the problem escalates with Lofty threatening to jump the bar and Tezza holding him back more worried that the old fool will do himself a mischief or the barman will be hammering seven bells of shit out of him.

The manager is called to settle the dispute, and the pair is persuaded to calm down by security as the manager approaches. Tezza suddenly sits upright on his stool and speaks.

"Lofty, Lofty, look its fucking Spider. He says

"Well stuff me so it is" says Lofty as the well-dressed slightly balding old shipmate struts purposefully toward the barman at the other end of the bar.

It wasn't long before the manager; Spider recognised the pair and with a couple of words to the barman beers arrive and Spider settles down for a catch-up chat with lads in a booth. Some hours later after many free beers and discussions Spider who it turns out owns the place as well as manages it offers the boys the bridal suit at the same cost as the basement room and looks forward to seeing them at the Vets convention ball on Saturday night.

As that was a no brainer the boys quickly move their stuff to the palatial suite on the 14th floor with wonderful beach and ocean views.

"This is the life eh mate" says Lofty.

"Yep, but the only problem is how are we going to sort this out with the wives as to which one of us moves out of here." says Tezza

"Tezza, Tezza, Tezza, you really are getting old. Mate, you and I are going to stay here and let them believe we are in the basement room. That way they will feel victorious, and we can enjoy another day or so of peace, luxury and quiet." Says Lofty with a triumphant look on his face

The rest of the afternoon passed peacefully with the two old mates shooting the breeze and enjoying the luxury of the bridal suite. They seemed to get a lot of attention from the overtly gay room service guy who thought he had come across some birds of a feather. Lofty's impersonation of a gay guy perhaps helped as there seemed to be an endless supply of food and drink

Later in the afternoon Tezza notices a large cruiser pulling up to the nearby wharf with the two wives stepping off and heading for the hotel. The lads had already left a message for the ladies, arranging a meeting time and place for the departure to the Friday night.

At the appointed hour the concierge arrived with the car and a disgusted look on his face as the lads waited in the foyer for the wives. Handing them a note which said they can no longer park in the basement due to the state of their car, the concierge hurries away expecting violence from the pair as he had heard about the banana bar incident.

The fronted both the men individually and had some terse words about the motel they had been booked into and how long it took the lads to get here as well as complaints from Lofty's neighbours re the motorised behemoth exploit and other stuff along the way that had been reported in regional papers they had read. There's no doubt about the female grapevine, hope Dave's Missus isn't on it thinks Tezza.

After calming down the wives agree to head off to the meet and greet still complaining about the Shady Rest motel. Walking out into the forecourt Tezza opened the passenger doors of the hire car for the 2 ladies who reeled back holding their noses at the stink.

"Lofty, where's my car. You were supposed to be coming up in my little car. I know you tried to get that bloody behemoth of a thing on the road didn't you." says Loftys missus

Looking a bit sheepish, Lofty fesses up and explains the hire car.

"Good thing I asked Polly to keep an eye on you that morning. You're bloody lucky you're both not in jail." She continues

Lofty looks at Tezza with a knowing smirk that Lofty and Tezza's Mrs. pick up on instantly as women do.

"OK what did you do and how much is it going to cost us this time." Says Tezzas wife

"Nothing dear; we just had a couple of little misunderstanding on the way up" says Tezza without alluding to the restaurant episodes and other run ins with the law.

Opening the door to the hire car the ladies reel back.

"Look guys we are here for a good weekend, but we are not getting in that thing, it stinks in there. God knows what you've been up to or what the hire company will charge you when you return it." Says Loftys wife

"No doubt about it, we can't let you two out of our sight for 5 minutes can we, I hope we can expect to hear the full story at some stage over the weekend, but for now lets get to the meet and greet but not in that stinky thing" says Tezzas Mrs. with Mrs Lofty's. nodding in agreement.

Whilst awaiting their taxi, the lads tried to do some bribery to offset the bedroom tax that had been applied. The offer of gifts fell on deaf ears despite pointing out the handbag and clothes shop in the foyer the ladies had none of it. The pair of intrepid adventurers who are under no misapprehension they were back under the thumb again for the weekend as they head off to the Friday night meet and greet at the Vets convention.

Tezza had made sure that if anyone checked they were still residing in the basement room and not the Bridal suite. Just as well because the tone of the conversation with the ladies was hostile and the lads accommodation upgrade would only complicate things further.

On the other hand, the ladies seemed pleased that the lads were doing there penance in the basement room and it was also clear that neither of the lads would be enjoying any marital bliss over the weekend.

"That went well I think" says Lofty smiling as they walked into the convention centre behind the wives

"You reckon, there's I think there's something wrong as my missus would never turn down the opportunity to spend money on handbags and stuff" says Tezza with a quizzical look on his face.

"What is it with handbags mate. I've never been able to work out why they need so many of them" says Lofty

"Ah, glad you asked. Once we get settled and the wives take off to catch up with their cohorts I will give you the whole truth behind handbags before they get back." Says Tezza with a knowing look.

THE LEATHER TARDIS

Sipping his beer and reclining in the plush leather chair in the convention centre bar Tezza opens discussions on womens handbags.

Lofty, I promised to update your knowledge on the handbag thing. To me a woman's handbag is a leather Tardis.

Lofty looking puzzled says,

"you mean like Dr who and his time machine."

"Yep says Tezza, on the outside it's a police phone booth. Step through the door and it's bigger than a block of flats."

"I think I know where this is going but carry on."

"Ok, the leather Tardis or handbag is a much more interesting piece of apparatus than Dr who's piece of crap. Carried by women mainly, they seem to contain all manner of things. Most of the contents will be familiar to you having seen them regularly disgorged onto the nearest flat surface. However, their use and meaning has long been lost on me as I only carry one wallet which seems to keep me content for years.

"My wallet has become an old friend that cuddles up to my hip pocket or inside my jacket.

Lofty pipes in with his considered opinion.

"Yes, I get that, they are like my Flano, somewhat ragged and worn around the edges, with the occasional spilt food stain ground in. Some even have the telltale circle of birth control devices embedded on their skin from past adventures that never happened. They often smell like old bus seats (if you're into a wallet sniffing that is) and look like they have been to a free beerfest."

"Correct on says Tezza. The one rule we men have is to never buy a new one until the old one is either lost on a noteworthy night out or simply falls apart. The exception to this, of course, is the well-meaning wife who gives you one for Christmas (wallet of course). You are duty bound now to try and lose it or find a reason to give it to your least favorite relative and disclaim any knowledge of the disposal.

"Hang on a minute, I wondered why you gave me a wallet last Christmas, Tezza I gave it to my son, who then gave it to his mate for a birthday present." says Lofty

"Looks like my theory is proved then" says Tezza with smirk on his face.

"OK, says Tezza, let's get down to the bones of the problem. Whilst most of us mere males have but one wallet that lasts for decades there are of course the new age types letting the side down with one of those awful manbag things that women try to saddle us with.

Lofty jumps on that comment,

"your spot on mate, and my sister-in-law tried to cajole me into one. It was a close call I can tell you."

"Well my observation is that Man bags have pretty much died out, but you still see the occasional one of these clutched fervently by an embarrassed male with a wife proudly showing how she has changed her once macho man into a bag carrying .... Well, you know what I mean

"So back to the leather tardis says Tezza. Womenfolk have dozens and dozens of handbags to match every sort of possible combination of apparel. To see the variety and logic of this you need to follow a lady into her dressing area (you may need permission to do this by the way) and watch the parade of what fits with what."

"I've been excluded from that pleasure for years," Lofty says.

Continuing his lecture Tezza expands on his theory

"My theory is that had men been in charge when these leather tardis's /handbags were designed we would have simply added a couple of pockets to the Bra. Problem solved although the lumpy bits might not have been so appealing if the ladies tried to cram all their junk into their bra pockets (I still might patent that idea someday)

"Brilliant I could even see the garage door opener built into the left nipple spot" says Lofty

"OK let's not get ahead of ourselves says Tezza cutting Lofty off at the pass and continuing his lecture on handbags.

"The one thing you can be sure of is these bloody things contain all manner of things. You can bet there will be everything from parking tickets to lipstick and makeup as well is the odd change, bus tickets and all sorts of odds and sods used in manipulating the woman's face or painting stuff on it. They never seem to be cleaned out and I'm sure there is a lost tribe living in my wife's bag as every time I go near it, I get speared by something inside. There are also hundreds of pockets in some of them, like little apartments for stuff to live in. I often wondered if the handbag needs feeding or refueling sometimes."

"Maybe that's a secret women's business." Says Lofty trying not to interrupt Tezza entertaining flow

"A word of warning here Lofty. If you're ever asked to go and find something in one of these mystery caves, trust me, you'll not be able to locate it or anything else. I think this is a female security test to see if they have properly disguised the contents from male eyes."

"Ahh!, secret women's business again, eh?" Says Lofty

"Trust me, you will look, and you'll look but it will not be where you think it is because they have secret pouches and zippers and little things inside to hide things that you will never find. Then, of course, there is that lost tribe that will spear you if you get too close. When asked to go and look in a handbag make an excuse, any excuse but get out of it because it will only end in tears and questions about your sanity being asked. She, however, will go straight to the spot where the thing is and you'll be made to look foolish in front of whoever she wants to impress."

"I see you know my missus then I guess the lesson from all this is that women have multiple leather tardis's to carry with them for all types of occasions. Most men have a single wallet" says Lofty

"You've got it right. We mere males must live with the fact that women have these leather bags with all the stuff in them which is vital to their existence and all the mysteries that go along with them. It doesn't mean we have to emulate them by buying a man bag ourselves. Stick with the old wallet containing the predictable credit cards and a photograph of the kids, a bit of money when you're allowed to have some other meaningful, manly stuff.

"The lesson from all of that is. Don't buy a man bag whatever you do, but you must be aware of their ploys to get you into one." Says Tezza

THE MEET AND GREET SESSION

"I sometimes wonder why I attend these dreary events" says Lofty as they stand in line to register

"What are you on about, this is the first one you've been to in 6 years or more. Says Tezza.

"Yeh, your right, I suppose I should support these veteran things but it's so depressing." He says

The check-in desk is full of volunteers giving each attendee a handout bag full of information on incontinence, bowel problems, dementia and all the things you don't need to be reminded about on a fun weekend. Grabbing the bag full of stuff, the discussion progresses about the last convention they attended together as they head into the meeting area with the wives trailing behind chatting to other wives they knew from previous events.

The opening event of all the Vets conventions in the past was always the Friday night meet and greeting sessions. It seemed to Tezza that this event was organised to let individuals gauge how much their fellow vets had deteriorated and to give the Politicians a chance to glad hand their way around the room and have something to put in their tedious newsletters

There's a beer issue at the door and everyone proceeds to get drunk as skunks while some fool from the Govt. health Department stands up and lectures us on kidney and liver diseases. Mind you nobody but his cheer squad could hear what he had to say as the free beer, wine and spirits was disappearing at an alarming rate. So much for liver disease.

The pair circulate and meet up with some old mates until finally heading back to the bar for a top up and find a quiet corner out of the politicians radar range.

"Lofty, you know I like a good old 'do you remember story' as much as the next guy. But I've heard the same stories about 30 times over the years. It appears many of our old comrades in arms have never moved on or have made a life built around alcohol and golf." Says Tezza

"Your very ungracious mate. Your probably right Chief says Tezza but as you so rightly pointed out it's been 6 years since I've been to one of these but I agree it looks like nothing has changed."

Tezza, thinking for a moment suggests an example as they moderate their beer intake seeing the ladies looking their way with that don't get pissed and you might get lucky look

"It's the usual old fools banging on about how good it was when and blah blah blah. Sorry guys, it wasn't all that good running around freezing our arses off in the arctic. Oh that's right... you guys were based in Malta or Greece weren't you? Have you noticed how quickly they disappear to harass someone else, medals clanging angrily as they stomp off. It's that sort of stuff that bores me mate concludes Tezza.

"Ok old mate let's have a good day tomorrow and look forward to taking the ladies to the AGM ball" says Lofty as they decide to call it a night and head back to their hotel with the ladies in tow.

On the way back the ladies make a point of telling the lads how good their room was and how they planned to have a nightcap on their 7th floor balcony overlooking the bay. Lofty and Tezza pretend to be hurt and jealous knowing this would work in their favour but also knowing full well they had a bottle of champers on ice awaiting them in the 14th floor luxury suite.

SHOPPING PROTOCOLS FOR MEN

Sitting on their balcony sipping champagne the lads mused over the day. Lofty is still bemused by the ladies handbag theory and decides to open a discussion on shopping.

"Our discussion on ladies handbags led me to think about mend protocols for shopping. I probably should explain this is secret mens businesses so don't tell your Missus. " Says Lofty

Continuing his thoughts Lofty is on a roll

"This is how it goes. Firstly, I know that you (generally) love sport and either playing or watching it mate, no matter what they try to tell you shopping is not a sport OK!! says, Lofty

Tezza jumps right into the discussion,

"As I get older, Ive learned to resist less and agree more. Thus, a trip to the shops with my wife is best left 'resistance free' in my experience."

" Now you're getting ahead of yourself again Tezza, if we grumble about going shopping, they, (women) get aggressive and dogmatic. As tempting as it is to respond to the negative, I believe if you use any of the following you will immediately incur the bedroom and food tax. For instance, don't respond to their questions like

"You want me to look beautiful don't you" with the common cry. We have beer for that. Or "you want to eat don't you" We have pub grub and fast food outlets for that. Or "don't you want the house clean" we have .... Maybe I won't go there.

"Alright smarty, what's the answer" says Tezza

Drawing breath between his teeth and trying to look sincere Lofty launches into his solution.

"Smart men know that resistance is futile, and compliance has its benefits. If your missus has just had a successful trip to the mall, I bet you're comfortably watching a sports show on TV while she busies herself trying on all the junk she just bought and calling her friends with the news.

"Thats low resistance gets rewarded. I bet you even got a nice dinner and had a beer brought to you. Come on fess up, you did, didn't you "says Lofty

OK, OK says Lofty, you're right, I've tried both but agree the low resistance approach paid off the best.

See, that's how we men cope. We go to the mall, make appropriate noises, pretend to admire garments and be careful not to stare at the attractive young thing in the Bra department (viz Chevy Chase film) while avoiding the inevitable question "does my bum look big in these' You know we can't answer that question... ever.". says Lofty peering over the top of his glasses at Tezza.

"Even though he managed to avoid the Man bag and resisted the face cream male makeover solutions offered whilst checking out the good-looking females in the cosmetics section, the wife is content that she has molded her fella into a new age man and thus she strives to make him feel appreciated for his considerate ways.

"Meanwhile, we fellas have had a hassle and whinge free sortie to the female heartland (the Mall) and now reap the benefits of a nice dinner; a beer delivered to our man couch and complete control of the remote for a few hours. Who knows even a bit rumpy-pumpy is on the cards if the garments purchased are at all inspiring."

"So, it's a win-win" says Tezza.

"Yep, but for God sake don't tell the sisterhood or they'll cotton on to our ploy for a happy life. says Lofty,

Best we go get some rest as we have the dreaded shopping trip with the wives in the morning says Lofty heading off to bed

After a good night's rest and making peace with the wives by going shopping with them in some god-awful bazaar the following day, the foursome prepares to attend the not to be missed AGM and Grand Ball.

THE VETS CONVENTION

A rriving in style on the Saturday evening in a Limo ordered by the ladies and looking like a pair of overdressed penguins with the ladies proudly on their arms they enter the venue and send the wives off to find their seats in the dinner area and to catch up on gossip with other wives and partners they know from days past.

Meanwhile the lads enter the meeting room next to the grand ballroom in time to find their seats for the Annual General Meeting (AGM) that always precedes the dinner and dancing part of the evening.

The AGM was typical of previous ones with the assembled hangovers trying to wrestle with the usual smart-arse locker-room lawyer who always seems to raise a point of order just as you're hoping to escape the tirade of argument and blithering. Finally, the thing is over and as usual nothing has been resolved except the date and venue for the next piss up (read AGM). Into the bar head the lurching, fumbling assembly of well-meaning vets for another couple of hours of drinking as a warmup to the evening's dinner dance.

THE GRAND BALL

The dinner dance.... that not to be missed event. The vets all decked out in ill-fitting suits and tuxedos that have seen better days. The occasional overzealous ironing marks here and there and the odd food stain from last year's lasagna. The ladies, God bless them have tried to outdo each other's Kmart Fashion and Payless footwear. The occasional over exposed aging bosom raises nothing more than an eyebrow now but never goes unnoticed by the ever-present waitress harassers in the assembly.

The tables have been carefully set out to ensure the lads are sitting with a bunch of complete strangers with strange habits and hobbies. Tezza had couple of new age Buddhist converts, a couple who collect beer cans whilst Lofty sat next to a lady who makes clothing out of dog hair. None of these folk were vet's past or present (thank god) but had been civilian support people with some affinity to military service.

Smiling politely, Lofty and Tezza sit through discussions on the difficulties of procurement of military latrines and the efficiency of garbage disposal units whilst trying to eat some cold compote of jellied something, until it was time for the speeches.

"Oh how I hate these," say Tezza leaning over to Lofty

Twenty minutes of backslapping and congratulations to the usual suspects (the ones who always seem to be glued to clipboards and wear armbands) and its time for the guest speaker.

In the meantime some gluttonous stodge arrives masquerading as chicken ala king. More like King Kong flambé thinks Lofty. So, to the sound of false teeth chattering on the inedible stodge, the occasional rude noise from the deaf old vet at the next table who keeps asking his equally deaf wife 'what'd he say' and somebody throwing up in a bucket at the back, we have the local member for parliament flapping his gums.

Lofty notices the speaker was having some difficulties with the presentation and says,

"Oh Joy, his power point presentation doesn't work, and maybe he'll go away.

"No, wait he's a politician and they don't go away, ever says Tezza. As his wife tells him to be quiet and don't embarrass her

Through monotone meanderings and a sea of gobbly gook the speaker is finally finishedare finished with a well done and your country appreciated your efforts from the Polly who would not be old enough to shave yet.

Sweets arrived. The choice is really no choice but it depends on what color you like best. Tezza declined the stuff, as he couldn't work out if it was ice cream or duck livers or both. It certainly smelt like the latter. Lofty was told later it was treacle pudding by the deaf vet who managed to get his false teeth stuck in the stuff and had to have his equally deaf wife remove them for him. That was a wonderful conversation and explained the sticky stains on Lofties jacket.

During all this time the band is playing in the background, sounding more like a musician's fight using instruments as weapons, the compere (bloke with the loudest voice) announces that dancing has started and invites everyone to the floor.

A few hardy or drunk souls venture out and try to do a Cha Cha to rock around the clock or something similar. There is always the smartarse who knows how to dance and is convinced they are the centre of the whole evening as they and his partner sweep around the floor missing all the swaying and clomping drunks.

They're show is for the entire assembly on how it should be done sweeping around the floor in true ballroom style. This of course does not go unnoticed by the wives who as per usual comment on Lofty and Tezzas lack of dancing skills

"See, that's how it's done, why can't you dance like that". says Tezzas wife with Lofties nodding agreement

"My undies aren't that tight love" says Tezza as he and Lofty consider heading off to the bar leaving their wives to ponder his response. But the look they get tells them it's not a good idea and they decide to sit it out for the time being.

In the meantime more free wine arrives with Lofty being regaled with the details of how to make a jacket from his dog's fur and Tezza is being converted to Buddhism. To escape the both Tezza and Lofty get up to dance just as the bands tempo changes and the MC for the night thinks he will try his hand at singing Sinatra style.

The dancing was good and probably the only time in recent memory they had held their wives in their arms and had them rest their heads on their shoulders during the slow shuffle stuff. It seemed like a duty at first but as it progressed both men began to relive their courting days and the love they had for their wives.

The pair with wives in hand shuffle around the floor to the awful cacophony avoiding the collapsed drunks at the edge of the floor (maybe they were dead? Who knows) and run into Spider Webb, Dave and Jumper and they collectively decide to escape to the nearby public bar for a quiet drink. On the way Tezza checks with Spider and Dave to ensure they are okay with the collective story. Dave assures Tezza that he has taken the blame and Spider just Blinks.

After an hour or so and a couple of rounds of drinks they decide to go back for the last dance with the ladies. Arriving back an hour or so later the place has deteriorated considerably.

2 old vets take swings at each other in one corner whilst their partners hold them back. Empty bottles litter the tables; there's a chorus of rude songs being belted out in the other corner. The band went to ground after the sax player apparently got it on with the trombonist's wife out the back. There are a bunch of bodies propped up in a corner where it looks like they have been dragged. 2 women are fighting over some aging vet who must have had a history with one or both 40 years ago.

The scene was not conducive to anything except going home. Thus, Tezza and Lofty decide with the lady's concurrence to retreat to their hotel which is thankfully not a long way away from the main venue and the mayhem. A nightcap is enjoyed by them and the guys get a cuddle for their efforts tonight which they take as a positive sign that they may be forgiven.

THE LONG ROAD HOME

The wives had made it quite clear that they were never going to allow the lads to make the trip back home on their own. Furthermore, the hire car looked like it was on its last legs and having been banned from the hotels underground car park following complaints from visitors and guests, it looked like a big bill was coming. At one stage someone had called the police suspecting there was a dead body in the back so it had been moved by the hotel staff and had sat out in the tropical sun festering away all weekend.

The convention had well and truly ended and goodbyes were made on the Sunday morning as the foursome sat down to breakfast. Clearly the women had a plan in mind by the way they sat like a jury at murder trial.

Tezza's wife set out the rules.

"Firstly, after we check out you're going to take the car somewhere and clean the thing up as best you can and return it to the hire company, and hopefully they will take it back."

Working as a chastising committee of two Lofty's wife then carries on the instructions,

"you're to meet us at the airport at 3.0pm as you two are flying home with us and that's not negotiable, right"

"So where are you ladies going between then and now" says Tezza, with a look of interest on his face.

Leaning across the table with a menacing look on her face, Tezza's wife answers the question

"None of your business but seeing as you're paying for it we are off to a spa this morning and then some shopping before we leave for the airport. Your job is just to be at the airport at 3.00pm and we will have your tickets. If you aren't there, you're on your own getting home. Got it"

Nothing changes, thinks Tezza as the wives stomp off to the reception desk.

Turning to lofty with query he asks:

"Do you think we should tell them we've been living in the Bridal suite for the last few days?" says Tezza, feeling a bit remorseful.

"Don't be silly, I had it all fixed up with Spider and believe you me those women of ours checked out our room number and probably had a bloody good laugh into the bargain thinking we were living in the basement. Mate it's important that what happens on the road stays on the road right!"

With that the lads headed to the coffee shop for a heart starter coffee with rum in it and a Tezza's favourite sticky bun.

THE RUB A DUB DUB CAR WASH

The local car wash was quieter than usual for a Sunday morning as the boys drove in with all the windows open to try and dispel the smell and a trailing band of dogs behind them. Tezza got out and fiddled with the coin slot car wash pylon whilst Lofty in the passenger seat sat reclining half asleep at the start of the automatic carwash.

"Ive almost got used to the stink in here Tezza," says Lofty pulling his bucket cap down over his eyes

Suddenly the car lurches forward toward the whirling brushes and jets of water. Lofty fumbled in vain for the ignition keys but it appears Tezza had taken them out of the ignition when he got out to read the instruction plate and put the money in the slot.

There was no getting out of the car now as it disappeared into the tunnel of whirling brushes and jets of water. Lofty decided his fate was sealed and pulled his bucket hat further down over his eyes as jets of water flooded into the car along with soap and flailing brushes.

A man could get drowned in here thought Lofty as Tezza furiously pushed buttons in an effort shut the thing down. There was a bang and whirring sound from inside the car wash and the whole thing came to a halt except for the water and soap jets. It appeared one of the brushes had managed to get caught in a seat belt and seized the whole thing up. The attendant rushes up to Tezza saying, what you do what you do in a distinct Asian accent.

Whilst Tezza argued the case with the increasingly aggressive attendant Lofty was planning his escape from the car filling with water? He remembers reading about kicking out the windscreen somewhere so that's what he did as the side doors and windows were blocked by the big brushes.

The sound of shattering glass sent the attendant ballistic. I call the police, you in big trouble now. He yells heading back to the office

Meanwhile Lofty crawled out from between the brushes and freed the jammed brush which started the whole thing off again. The flooded car, minus windscreen and with big foot marks all over the bonnet finally emerged from the end of the tunnel.

The lads jumped in the half-flooded car and sped off with water pouring out of every orifice and glass everywhere.

"Well, that's another fine mess you've gotten us into Ollie" says Lofty. Doing his best Laurel and Hardy impersonation.

"Me! It was your stupid idea to bring the bloody thing to the car wash. I wanted to take it to the detailer near the hotel but Oh no, that will cost way too much, now look what's happened." Says Tezza as they speed away in the wrecked car.

They continue to argue for a short time about Lofty's penny pinching and Tezza's techno phobia until every argument is exhausted.

"Maybe the wives are right mate perhaps we shouldn't be let loose in public." says Tezza,

The pair then turn to each other and start to giggle like a pair of naughty schoolboys.

"Yep, but our problem now is getting this thing through the hire car company's scrutiny". says Lofty

"No, it's not the only problem. All the baggage is in the boot including the wives clothes shopping after you assured them you would bring it all out in a cab. By now it will all be a sodden mess and probably smell worse than the car did." Says Tezza

"Shit I forgot all about that. Sorry, I thought I was saving a couple of bucks". says Lofty

"That's not all take a look at us." says Tezza,

The pair looked down at their clothes which were of course soaked and shrinking (Cheapo specials) in the heat of the afternoon sun.

As luck would have it the hire company local outlet at the airport was managed by one of the Vets from the convention and after some smooth talking about kangaroos and riverbed crossings etc the car was returned but with a hefty penalty to follow in the mail.

As Tezza suspected, the suitcases in the back were all full of water. The hire company refused to handle them so there was no choice but to see if the airline would take them. Heading to the departures area they left a trail of dirty smelly water behind as they crossed the road into the airport with amazed looks from passengers turning to see the pair pass by like a pair of overweight AFL players in their shrunken clothing pushing stinking suitcases on a luggage trolley.

Lofty had pulled his bucket hat down as far as it would go and Tezza had done likewise with his baseball cap. At least they were on time for once thought Lofty

Suddenly a familiar voice stops them in their tracks.

STOP RIGHT THERE

Y OU TWO, STOP RIGHT THERE!

The sound of an angry woman came from behind them. It was unmistakably Tezza's wife. As the pair turned around, they were confronted with 2 very angry women heading their way and trying to avoid the puddles the boys were leaving behind them.

What the hell have you two been up to now? Look at you both. Your clothes have shrunk and you look like overweight versions of AFL players. says Tezza's Mrs.

Lofty's wife adds to the dialogue.

"This would be your fault I'm guessing you silly old fool she says prodding Lofty in the chest.

Tezza jumps to Loftys defence,

"No it's all my fault you see........

Cutting him off mid-sentence Tezza's wife slaps two tickets onto Tezza's chest

"Never mind here's your tickets go and book the luggage in if they will take it and we will see you both at home at our place, you've both got some explaining to do when we get home."

The airline refused to take the soaking luggage. After some discussion they were referred to a freight forwarder who had it all shrink wrapped and forwarded at a huge expense of course.

"Let's not tell the ladies" Says Tezza.

"Good idea mate let's make it a surprise" and they begin giggling again.

It soon became apparent when boarding the aircraft that the ladies were sitting toward the front whilst the lads were seated down in the back row of seats away from other pasengers. Clearly, the wives were embarrassed by the lads and did not even make eye contact with them except for one frosty look when they passed down the aisle. Other passengers gave the lads a variety of funny looks and giggles as they made their way down the aisle.

Once in the air and the drinks trolley came around, Tezza orders a couple of beers and the pair settle back to reflect.

"Well mate that was one hell of trip wasn't it. says Lofty

"Sure, but I think both our bank balance will take a hammering in coming days." says Tezza

"So, it was worth it. Skol" says Lofty clinking his bottle with Tezzas as they both put on their headphones and put their seats back.

After downing the rest of their beers, the pressures of the day took their toll and the pair slipped into a deep sleep. The Mexican snacks they had eaten at the airport had a recurring effect on both men giving them substantial gas. However, now asleep and with their headphones on both men were oblivious to the the fact that the noisy smelly farts had caused the flight attendant to come to the back of the plane to see if everything is Ok.

The noises and smells they were emitting was cusing other passenger distress and discomfort

ROW 27 EXCURSIONS

Tezza awakes with a start from his slumber to find the flight attendant standing over him with a mask on.

"What are you doing, I'll have another beer please" says Tezza in his half-awake state, and so will he.

The wives, fearing that their hubbies might have got into trouble again have headed back to see what the fuss is all about.

"Geeeeez Tezza, was that you" says Tezza's wife.

After some discussion and spraying toilet deodorant around the flight attendant reseated as many of the passengers as she could away from the two men. Leaving the deodorant spray handy she warned the two men to control themselves or they may be arrested when they land.

The turmoil over and the names taken the pair settle back for the rest of flight with a whole section to themselves after most of the passengers moved forward to escape the smell which seemed to linger.

"Mate I was just thinking about what they would charge us with as the trolley dolly had threatened" said Lofty

"let me see, your honour the pair are charged with unlawful discharges of noxious gas from their backsides" says Tezza, turning to Lofty as the pair begins giggling again.

"Let's do it again sometime mate says Lofty,

"Absolutely but we've got to get home first and face the music". says Tezza

More laughter as the pair sat back and relaxed satisfied that they had a good time but still dropping the occasional fart defined by the spraying of deodorant.

The flight back home was mostly uneventful except for the pungent odour that the two old rascals left in the back two rows of the aircraft. The plane finally touched down in Sydney and the usual rush to get off was accelerated by the stink at the back. As seasoned travelers Lofty and Tezza knew the game and how it was played. The rat race toward the exit was mostly thinning out so the lads gathered their courage and looked back toward the rear of the aircraft as they walked up the aisle.

Not surprisingly the atmosphere around the 2nd last row appeared to resemble the sky just before a massive storm was about to break as they followed the crowd quietly wondering if they would be arrested or if not what the trip home in the car would bring and whether the Airline would hit them with a cleanup bill for their gastric excursions due to their over indulgence at the Mexican food café whilst waiting to board.

Both knew the trip home in the car would not be a pleasant trip. Arriving in the baggage collection area to the stares and whispers of their fellow passengers, the time-honoured farce of jostle and bad manners at the baggage carousel commenced

"I often wonder about people. Why all the worried faces and hassle. I wonder if they are all worried that their baggage might be getting giddy and sad going round and round on a carousel and wondering where their owners must be." Says Lofty,

"You think too much Lofty, we don't have any bags so let's get out of here before we get into any more trouble." Says Tezza dragging Lofty out toward the cab rank

Neither of their wives had spoken a word to them after their gaseous escapes on the plane. They seemed to have disowned them as they watched their wives depart in a limo as they waited in the taxi rank with everyone staring and the occasional giggle.

"All right for some" says Tezza referring to the wife's limo.

"Yeh mate, I think we are in deep shit this time." Said Lofty

Jumping into a cab that smelt like a 2-week-old kebab that had been stuck under someone's armpit, the lads headed home.

Tezza breaks the silence noticing Lofty with his head out the window like a dog catching air.

"Whilst you've been worrying about the increase in the bedroom tax I have been quietly thinking." Says Tezza

"That sounds dangerous but go on." says Lofty

"Right, this is how we play it, initially we will be given the cold shoulder and hot tongue menu, but we must cop it sweet and do the yes dear no, dear routine, later when the coven reaches for their short, broom sticks to belt us with and call us very naughty little boys we can commence our counterattack. Your part Lofty is to just follow my lead and for fuck's sake don't waiver." Says Tezza

Lofty, with his head back out the window again yells back.

"Mate, do you think I came down with the last rain shower, you haven't got a bloody clue have you, so following your lead should be easy, I will just sit there and look dumb founded as they beat us to death, alright?" he says

"Lofty you of little faith, trust me."

Tezza wondered what chance the plan would have if Lofty could see through it without even hearing what it was. Tezza was going to need all his acquired devious skills of lying and guile to extricate the boys from this one, but Tezza was always up to the challenge, and already conjuring the pieces of the plan.

HOME SWEET HOME, MAYBE

The wives had decided to make their own way home in a Limo leaving the boys isolated in the cab rank. This was the start of the mental cruelty program they had planned as payback. The two men's arrival home was as icy as a butcher's fridge and just as threatening. Having been sat down in Loftys lounge room like two naughty schoolboys outside the principal's office the ladies glared at them both shaking their heads and mumbling about being disgraced. Tezza broke the icy silence,

"Look ladies we are happy to take our medicine aren't we Lofty."

"Yes," mumbled Lofty not convinced he knew what the medicine was going to be. Tezza went on with that hung dog look he did so well while Lofty mirrored his posture,

"We know we stuffed up a bit and we want to make it up to you. A wary looked came across the wives' faces.

"Really" says Lofties wife knowing this was going to be good.

"OK, how will you make it up to us, and it better be good, says Tezza's wife

"Well, ah, ah" stumbled Tezza and just when he was about to reach for the ejection seat handle Lofty cut in,

"It's a secret at this stage isn't it Tezza,

"Yep that's it, it's a secret." Stumbles Tezza

In unison the girls quietly smiled whilst Tezzas missus exclaimed,

"well gents the cat had better be let out of the bag or you both know the consequences. Tezza went his usual deep shade of white when disaster approached and even the usual flamboyant Lofty in these circumstances was silent.

"Well, we are waiting." Says Loftys wife

Lofty looked at Tezza who was looking out the window towards the heavens for some divine intervention. Then noticing the back of a magazine on the table with an advert for Christmas cruises he had it solved, without any further consultation with his brain Tezza blurted out,

"a CRUISE." a crhristmas cruise to some exotic islands

Lofty gave every indication that he was about to choke.

"Ok but we need details, said the wives, rising out of their chairs and looking quite menacing.

Tezza sensed he was heading down a one-way street the wrong way with oncoming traffic and so again without consulting his brain he calmly said,

"We think a Christmas cruise would be nice" he said with some degree of confidence that sounded like there was a plan

"Ok but don't think your off the hook. We will be watching you both and that idiot mate of yours Sandy very carefully" says Tezza wife

As the women leave muttering to each other Lofty turns to Tezzay and quietly says,

"Mate that was brilliant but where did that come from".

"Don't know mate, just made it up as I went. I will bet it's going to cost us though."he said holding up the glossy magazine with the advert in it

"Well, at least we are off the hook so let's go visit Sandy and have a few beers and see what mischief he has been up to."

Walking up the road to Sandys place they notice the ladies talking with a tow truck driver and handing him a set of keys.

"What do you suppose that's all about" says Tezza. "No idea mate but I don't think it's anything good " says Lofty as they knock on Sandys door. The door opens and they are confronted by Sandy in a terrible state, all flustered and distressed.

"Guys, they are towing the beasty away, no more chariot of fire. I tried to stop them but the cops are involved so I had to let it go." said Sandy looking sad and dejected.

A pall of sadness fell over the threesome but several beers and many stories later they had put the loss behind them and were planning the Christmas Cruise.

The End – for now

check out book two, **The Twilighters Christmas Cruise** for more of Tezza and Lofty's adventures

About the Author

Thor Wesenlund

Thor's experience as submariner in the Australian Navy in the 60's and 70's influenced much of the content of this book. However, much of the content is derived from a long road trip with his lifelong friend Terry and the memorys that the trip raised. Thor's long history of tinkering and making stuff out of junk is also evidenced in parts of the story. Whilst the book is pure fiction, there are elements of truth hidden in the discussions as they have arisen in the past. The quirky, tongue in cheek philosphies often ring true with his age group. Im sure some will be offended but they can just get over it whilst the rest of us enjoy the read and dont take it too seriously.

Also from the same author

BEBE – Finding Love

Coming soon

BEBE 2 –Retribution

The Twilighter – Christmas Cruise

The Twilighters – Mission Improbable

From the same publisher

Coffee Maidz – by Zoana Valund

Australias Submariner Chefs